SMOKE & RUBBER

BURNOUT BOOK ONE

ADELL RYAN

Published by Upside Down Red Umbrella
First Edition: June 2020

Cover Art by Covers by Christian
Edited by G. Surley

CHAPTER ONE

Despite being taller than the average woman, I still can't reach the top shelf in my new walk-in closet. Box of old photographs in hand, I stretch onto my tiptoes and try to balance it along the edge before pushing it the rest of the way.

All hope is shattered when I miss my mark and the box dumps forward, contents pouring over my head and scattering around my feet.

My hands grip the sides, fingers digging into the cardboard, and my eyes blur. Arms trembling, I chunk the box into the depths of the closet before my legs give way and I fall to my knees at the center of the mess. For a heartbeat, the buildup of tears comes as a relief; my hazy vision prevents me from reliving each memory as I desperately pick up the pictures one by one and stack them neatly.

As soon as the photographs are in a carefully organized semi-circle of small piles in front of me, the dam barricading my tears begins to weaken. Every carefully placed stick and stone held together by the perfectly mixed mud springs a leak. Another heartbeat later, the entire thing completely bursts.

When I blink the tears away, Jude is sitting across from me, leaning against the wall with his head back as he stares up toward that damn shelf and tries to curb his own emotions. The box I had thrown in my moment of anger and frustration is beside him, every picture now carefully placed inside. Whether the cause of his arrival is due to my muffled crying or because he was somehow feeling the negative energy of my grief, I'm not sure.

After my shuddering breaths and sniffles no longer fill the tight space, he adjusts, and our identical dark-brown eyes meet, an equally identical heartbreak hanging silently between us. That fleeting moment is when his resolve ends, though. Jude leans forward, clasps my face between his hands, and gives me a kiss on top of my head before standing and leaving me to continue grieving alone — something we've both done in isolation quite often lately.

Half of my heart aches the moment my brother exits, wishing he'd stay just a bit longer, hug me a bit tighter, break alongside me a bit more. The other half lightens knowing his absence means we won't talk about our father — rejoices that words of his untimely and horrific death won't be exchanged.

Wiping the wetness from my cheeks, I finally stand. Rather than trying yet again — and failing — to hide the memorabilia on the shelf, I pick the box up and tuck it safely away on the floor in the far corner.

With a final shaky breath, I leave the closet, ready to unpack the next box. When I step back into my bedroom, movement in the doorway causes me to startle.

"Dammit, Porter! You scared me." My hand presses against my chest, hoping to quell the insistent pounding.

Jude's best friend, longtime family business partner, my ex-boyfriend, and our new roommate enters. I retreat backward. "Jude asked me to come check on you," he states. Again, he moves forward, and I take another step back.

That doesn't stop him, though. When the center of my back hits the closet edge, the corner of his lips tick upward in accomplishment.

I would like to point out that Jude was just here checking on me himself, but I choose a safer response instead: "Thank you. I… I'm fine. Just adjusting, you know." Shoving my hands into the pockets of my jeans, I drop my gaze.

Porter drags a finger across my forehead and brushes the hair out of my eyes before slipping it under my chin. With slight pressure, he reroutes my attention from the ground to his cold, blue eyes. "Always lying," he whispers. "You know you don't have to do that with me…" The rest of his fingers splay over my jaw, his grip tightens, and his mouth comes to my ear. Voice lowering to a mere breath, he threatens: "I know all your secrets anyway, and you'll do well to never forget that."

Jude didn't send Porter in here to check on me; he sent himself in here. Jude must have mentioned my little breakdown to him, and he took it upon himself to make sure he is available… should I need a distraction from my heartache.

Not only does Jude have no clue Porter is in here, imposing and threatening, there are a number of other things he is in the dark about, too. Like, for instance, the detail where his best friend had been fucking his baby sister ever since the day she turned eighteen and he could legally do so without being caught with his pants down harassing an underage girl.

Not that it didn't stop him from conditioning me while I was young and vulnerable the few years preceding my eighteenth birthday. Nothing much stops Porter from getting what he wants. Right now appears to be no different.

"Now, we're going to try this again." The tone and pitch of his voice returns to normal, and his grip on my chin loosens. "You miss your dad…" His fingertips spread over my cheek and push into my hair near my ear. Hearing mention of my father instantly brings back all the emotions I had worked so hard to leave in a puddle on the closet floor. "Let me help take your pain away," he whispers, dragging his thumb along my quivering bottom lip. A single tear drips from the corner of my eye as his mouth presses against mine and his tongue pries its way inside.

Fortunately for him, I'm just this side of stupid enough to let him get his way where I'm concerned. Because he's right about one thing at least… he knows my secrets…

…and I'll do whatever it takes to make sure they stay just between the two of us.

CHAPTER TWO

"**M**orning." Jude gives me a quick kiss on the top of my head while lifting one of my hands and brushing the handle of a hot mug against my fingers. "Sleep well the first night in your new room?"

I accept his offering but place the mug onto the counter just long enough to hop on top before picking it back up and cupping it with both palms. Before committing to conversation, I lift the warm drink to my face, tilt my nose over the rim, and inhale. "Mmmm," I hum appreciatively, blowing into the mug with my exhale. "Yeah... I slept fine. Once I get done unpacking everything, it'll feel more... me... though. How about you?"

Jude shrugs, his tired eyes meeting mine as he leans against the kitchen counter beside me. "Porter and I stayed up late trying to find some information on the local street scene."

My eyes roll toward the ceiling. "Ugh... I should have known you chose to move us across the country just for car stuff."

Jude chuckles, taking a sip of his own beverage. "Gotta pay the bills somehow, Remi. Would you rather I work a nine-to-five at a real estate office or pull overtime at that pizza place around the corner?"

"Yeah... Maybe." One of Jude's dark-brown eyebrows lifts. There's no way my brother is at a point yet to where he'd be willing to become a blue-collar worker. "Look, I guess... I don't know... maybe I thought — hoped — we'd leave all that back in Cali."

Jude sighs and places his mug behind him before turning and resting on his hip to face me. He squeezes my knee and gives me a soft smile. "Our inheritance won't last forever. The vehicle industry is where the money is for us. It's what we know. Right now, Porter and I are not in a position to change our wheelhouse. Why waste time topping pies when we can go ahead and start building a new empire here, hm?"

"But picture the possibilities:" — I turn on the dramatics, extending my arms outward to indicate the hypothetical scene in front of us — "Jude Delancey, The Gulf Coast's premier Real Estate agent. 'Take a ride, and he'll show you inside.'" Jude huffs and picks his drink back up. "Just think... billboards everywhere featuring you *and* your car. Right next to those scantily-clad bathing suit models; hell, I bet you could even get one of them to spread open on the hood for you. That might bring in a different type of client, though. You'd have the men trying to figure out a way to get inside the model, while their wives would be looking to get inside their new homes."

Jude laughs, and I ache to bottle it up so I can pop the top and listen to it anytime I need a reminder of what life was like before the madness. "Wow… just… wow. You've really thought this through, huh?"

"What! I'm… I'm offended. Bro, that was just off the cuff. Want to see what else I can come up with?" I place my drink down, clap my hands together, and rub my palms in a circle. Jude shakes his head and turns to the sink to rinse out his mug.

Our sibling moment is instantly ruined when Porter enters the kitchen, strawberry-blond hair sticking up all over the place. Eyes still glazed over with the remnants of sleep, he ignores us and heads straight to the cabinet closest to the refrigerator and selects a box of cereal before collecting the milk.

Jude, being the overall great guy he is, pulls a bowl out of one of the unpacked moving boxes on the floor and hurries to clean it off before a half-asleep Porter starts pouring his breakfast all over the kitchen island. He's been known to do it before.

Porter pops open the cereal and unrolls the plastic bag. Jude slides the bowl onto the table just as Porter begins to tilt the box. Cereal pieces clink into the glass bowl, and my brother lets out a sigh of relief, throwing me a wink. I press my lips together to stifle the oncoming chuckle.

Now that my drink is cool enough to consume, I pick it back up and take a sip, reveling in the warmth as it moves down my throat and pools in my belly.

As soon as Jude is done catering to Porter's inability to function in the morning, he returns to my section of the counter again. "So… joking aside…" he starts, darting a wary glance in my direction. "We want you on the payroll."

I am committed to taking the next sip of my drink when he reveals this information, and instead of flowing smoothly, the liquid catches in my throat. My cheeks puff out to compensate, preventing the attempted swallow from spewing everywhere. One of my hands comes to my mouth as a precautionary measure while I attempt choking down the obstruction. Only after I'm confident the liquid is safely inside me do I gasp in a recovery breath. "Y-you want me in the business? To… what? Be your bookkeeper? Fuck that. I'm not about to sit behind a desk all day either."

Jude presses his lips together and narrows his dark eyes at me. "Don't pretend like it's not in your wheelhouse, too." I throw my head back and mumble a string of expletives at the ceiling. "You know more about vehicles than most men do. Plus… you're prettier than we are. We don't want you to keep books, Remi. We want you on the field. Recruiting. Porter will hire one of those billboard models looking to make a buck on the side if we need a bookkeeper."

Porter rises from the dead, deciding this is the time to voice his business insight. "Recruiting?" he scoffs. "Try telling her the truth."

I raise an eyebrow at my brother, who typically has no trouble telling me the truth. Jude leans forward and slaps Porter upside the head. "It's called conversation, idiot. Maybe you should try it sometime." He then turns to me and curves his eyebrows inward. "I was getting there, swear."

The very fact that Jude is so honest and open sits heavy on my shoulders as Porter turns around, leans against the island, and his blue eyes alight on every inch of me as he casually adjusts his morning glory. Taking another sip of my drink, gaze falling to the liquid inside, the small ceramic mug becomes a temporary barricade to hide behind.

Jude continues his explanation. "We need help looking for a certain underground street racing club."

Well, well, well… color me curious. "You mean the infamous Jude Delancey and Porter Davis are… stuck?!" I gasp, bringing the mug to my lap. Since we moved from an area well-known for their underground street racing where both Jude and Porter had been involved in the scene, this indeed comes as a shock. "You know Dad didn't want me involved in all this stuff. That was your calling, not mine. Don't they use forums like the other clubs tend to do? Surely finding them shouldn't be too difficult. Plus, after you secure enough meetings with other players in the industry, someone is bound to mention racing."

"Right, someone will eventually say something… but that could take time. Too much time spent on this is what we are hoping to avoid. And, yeah, they use a forum, every serious street racing club does, but Porter and I can't afford to keep spending all day and night dealing with busywork when there are other things that need to be accomplished. So… we're hoping you'll take on the gig — try to poke around a bit, learn about the area. Most street racers are closer to your age anyway."

"What if I find them?" I ask. Porter's gaze continues to touch every inch of my bare skin, drifting between my legs where the mug rests. Realizing my mistake, I cross my previously open legs at the ankle and place the mug beside me instead.

"You dig deeper. Figure out what they're about, how much money they bring in, where they tend to meet, where they race, and who might be looking to branch out," Jude elaborates, and every word that falls from his mouth adds another pound of weight to my already heavy shoulders.

"So, instead of creating your own club… you're… what?… planning a takeover?" I huff, crossing my arms over my chest.

"See," Porter pipes in, "I told you she was fucking perfect for the job."

Oh… I see… so this is Porter's genius idea.

Growing up in the shadows of the vehicle industry, I know just enough to understand where this is headed. As for field experience, though, I always steered clear of that part.

"We're not playing with toy cars anymore, Remi," Jude says with a sigh. "Months… we'll be broke in months. Go big or go home, right? And we sure as hell don't want to go *home*."

Porter's gaze finally leaves my body, moving to my eyes instead. "I was just telling Jude last night that there was no way you'd turn down the job. Not when having to work forty-hour-plus weeks is your other alternative."

Porter knows damn well I would work a minimum wage job any day over doing the underhanded shit they're proposing. But his first sentence underlined what he really meant: I am not being given the option to decline.

CHAPTER THREE

The words and images on the computer screen start morphing into swirls of colors. I blink fast to clear my rapidly clouding vision, but it only helps for a couple clicks of the mouse before the images blur again.

Porter and Jude were right: this apparent street racing club is well hidden. An indicator, unfortunately, that they are likely a significant player — if not *the* main player — in the local car scene and underground street racing circles. What's even more curious, is that I can't find anything hinting toward smaller clubs either. It's almost as though this invisible entity has completely monopolized the area's recreational vehicle clubs in general.

Challenge accepted, boys.

You can try to hide, but I'll find you.

Almost 90 percent of the time, a lack of information means there's something big hidden. The trick is finding the tinder.

I lean back in the office chair, close my eyes, and stretch my arms over my head, yawning. When my eyes open again, they land on the framed panoramic print Jude had strategically hung above his multi-screen computer setup. Lips curving downward, my gaze falls on the happy teenaged girl and her doting father.

As soon as Jude took the picture he swore he would print it big and keep it in his office. He never did. Until now. It was my sixteenth birthday; Dad and I were standing around my first — and only — vehicle. I have refused to drive anything else since the day he gifted it to me.

"Ride smart, Remi. There's no way in hell I would've given your brother a motorcycle when he was sixteen. I'm doing this because I tru—" A rock lodges in my throat, and I swallow hard, shaking the image and conversation out of my mind.

So much has changed since that day. Now all that remains is a broken girl and her trusty bike.

These past few days without her, while the transport company takes their sweet time delivering our vehicles, have only served to worsen the agony festering in my heart.

With a sigh, I drop my gaze, refusing to allow the memory to weasel its way into my heart anymore than it already has. Instead, I lean my elbows on each side of the multi-colored keyboard, rub the blur out of my eyes, and refocus on the screen.

One discussion after another eventually led to a particular forum — surprise, surprise. Certain this is the one, I pore over every thread and every comment a dozen times. The only thing that seems even remotely odd is a post that says:

:grub4close:

Every time I scroll through, my eyes catch on that one. Its randomness in addition to how many thumbs up reactions it has received since being posted just a few days ago, doubles my curiosity. The poster's profile photo is a drawing of a black crow on a white background.

Desperate for some sort of progress, I open a new browser tab and type in "crow gulf coast" on a hunch. Much to my surprise, the first listing that comes up is for *The Crowbar and Grill*. Leaning back in the chair, I let out a heavy breath and tap my fingers against the armrest.

Grub4close. Grub4close. Grub4close.

Hmm.

Since it's a combo bar and restaurant, I quickly surmise "grub" must indicate the restaurant part which, of course, segues to the thought that perhaps by "close" they plan to meet when the restaurant closes, which isn't at all unusual for car clubs.

My eyes track to the top right corner of the screen where the time and date display.

Today is the third…

Tomorrow is the fourth…

Perhaps the number four in the post means they are meeting tomorrow. The sound of my hands clapping together once echoes throughout the partially empty room.

Hell, even if I'm wrong at least it gives me something to do.

After all… how does that saying go?

Where there's smoke… there's rubber.

* * *

SLEEP DOESN'T COME EASY despite how exhausted I am after shutting down and crawling into bed. I toss and turn, my mind half-dreaming, half-mulling over everything going on. Occasionally the two intermix, and a bizarre half-breed reel plays. As soon as things turn dark, though, I shoot up in bed, sweat covering my forehead and heart threatening to pound out of my ribcage.

That's how I find myself in the kitchen far too early in the morning, mentally grousing that I now have to wait the entire day before The Crowbar and Grill's restaurant closes.

Come to find out, I am not alone in my inability to sleep. The streetlight filtering through the kitchen window outlines Jude's tall, filled-out frame. I ease up beside him quietly and lean my head on his shoulder.

His hand immediately comes up to my head and he presses my cheek against him tighter.

The small acknowledgments — a knee squeeze here, a kiss on the head there, brief hugs, shared silent moments — are the full extent of our mourning. We seldom speak of him — of why we left. Because doing so makes it too real. Too permanent. Too... risky.

"I think I found a clue." Even though I deliver the news as a whisper, it still seems overly loud in the late-night, early-morning silence.

"Of course you did," Jude states. "Never doubted you for a second."

As much as I disagree with what they're doing, the thought of letting Jude down — of disappointing him — in part drives my motivations; his approval and appreciation make all the other, more unpleasant, reasons easier to swallow.

Another thing I love about his approach is that he doesn't press or dig for information ahead of time. His mind works a lot like our father's in that way. Jude would prefer to wait until everything is wrapped up in one pretty package rather than it be delivered piece by piece for him to puzzle together.

Nothing more is said between us. The morning fast-forwards much like most mornings do. Porter wakes up and makes a mess in the kitchen before he and Jude convene to take care of business dealings.

The first part of the day is spent unpacking the rest of my stuff. Once that's done, my afternoon and evening hours are utilized doing a bit more precursory research. Including, but not limited to, creating new social media accounts.

When we'd planned to get the hell outta Cali, the step also came with a bit of an identity change. Not much, though. Going too overboard wasn't necessary. To keep things basic, both Jude and I started using our first names. Growing up, we were mostly referred to by our middle names per the request of our father once his business got big enough. We had also used the company name as our surname — again, as an added safety precaution. The company name, however, was short for our real last name, so we simply converted to utilizing our real last name once more.

While starting all my new social-circle profiles, I take a major leap and create an account in that forum. One of my favorite pastimes, in fact, is screwing with car guys. My go-to name? *DoubleD* — a play on my motorcycle's make and model, of course.

With the default image of a female avatar, it equates to instant fandom. Ugh… car guys.

Scratch that… ugh, guys in general.

Sure enough, as soon as my name pops up as "online," I get a personal message from HazerBeam:

:Welcome to the forum DoubleD. Let me know if you have any questions.:

One from PocketRocket comes in shortly after:

:Do ya keep dem puppies on a leash or let 'em loose?:

In response to HazerBeam, I type:

:Hey! Glad to be here. I'm looking to drop a flag. Can you point me in the right direction?:

The text cursor flashes as I hover my finger over the enter button. Eh… too forward, I decide, hitting the backspace button and choosing to ignore both messages instead.

CHAPTER FOUR

By the time I'm done screwing around on the forum, looking for information on past gatherings or anything along those lines — and failing — it's nearly time to head out.

For a girl who generally prefers to stay away from meets, I sure have a lot of car and racing paraphernalia: t-shirts and ball caps with snarky sayings, cycle-ready boots, things of those sorts.

For my sleuthing efforts, however, I decide to check things out in as unassuming a way as possible. Perfect messy bun, extra-skimpy shorts, and a baggy shirt. To top it all off, a smudge of pink lip gloss. Girly is a far cry from my usual, but sleuthing calls for a bit of pretend on my part.

If I wore what I generally prefer, they'd have me pegged as a street girl in a heartbeat. Besides, there's nothing that quite gets a car guy's motor running like the chance to break in a new toy — to talk about their vehicle with someone new and interesting. Or, really, to talk about their vehicle with anyone willing to listen.

"Headed somewhere?" Porter's voice punches through my thoughts. His big, burly body leans against my door frame, nearly filling the entire opening, eyes trailing from the flip-flops on my feet up to the bottom edge of my jean shorts.

The idea of wearing them so short seemed like a good one at the time, but having his gaze linger and darken during his inspection has me second-guessing my choice. I slip my hand behind the closet door and grab the first purse that touches my fingertips, not caring if it matches my outfit as long as I can hurry and get out of here.

I sling the purse's strap over my head, crossbody-style, swipe my phone and wallet off the bedside table, and hastily shove them inside its zippered opening. "Yeah, pretty sure I got a lead." I blow a puff of air out of the side of my mouth to move the stray hair from my eyes before finally meeting his scrutiny and stepping forward.

"Need a ride?" he asks as he steps aside to let me through.

"Ah, no thanks. I can take my bicycle; it's not too terribly far away. A bit farther than I would be willing to walk, but biking should be fine," I explain, making my way down the hall. "Any news on the car hauler?"

Jude, Porter, and I made the cross-country trip from Cali to Florida in Porter's Mustang, stopping through as many car shows and events as possible along the way. The rest of our vehicles, however, have yet to arrive.

"Tomorrow," he answers, stepping around and past me to push the glass sliding door open before I can reach out and do it myself. "Company said the truck got held up about midway."

"Oh, I bet Jude is pissed." I huff out a chuckle as I make my way off the deck and down the stairs. Once at the bottom, I tilt my head back, peering up at the stilted second story in search of Porter who is now leaning his elbows on the railing looking down at me. "My bet is that he gets a good chunk of money off the bottom line because of it, though."

"Already has," he affirms. "If they're not careful, I'm sure we'll find a way to *convince* them it's not worth the hassle to charge us at all."

The truth of that statement has me shaking my head in amusement as I wheel my bike out from beneath the deck. Both Jude and Porter were raised under Dad's wing; they learned how to work several facets of the vehicle industry quite well. That the transport company didn't bend over backward to deliver our vehicles sooner than promised is a shock in and of itself.

Eager to finish the small talk and leave Porter in a good mood, I hop on my bike, toe up the kickstand, and waddle it to the edge of the driveway. With a "See ya later," and quick wave over my shoulder, I pedal away.

* * *

THERE WAS MUCH TO BE DESIRED with the amount of sidewalks and biking lanes en route to The Crowbar and Grill, which is quite disappointing since this area is supposedly well-known as a tourist destination. You'd think they'd spend a bit of that hard-earned economic money to better cater to people who don't have motorized wheels.

Riding under the stars, I pass at least two other bicyclists on the way and am forced to veer into the car lane.

What's even more disappointing, though, is that there's not a boardwalk parallel to the beach in order for people to enjoy the sights. Instead, the beachside is filled with condominiums and restaurants. During the day, we can see the water from our new house but only through the sliver of space between high-rise residential buildings.

Fortunately, I arrive at The Crowbar and Grill unscathed. At least the restaurant has a bike rack. Before locking her in, I make a quick loop around the parking lot on the lookout for anything that might give these guys away.

The only vehicle that stands out, other than the occasional rental and soccer-mom van, is a late-eighties Monte Carlo. The Super Sport version if its spoiler and front fascia are any indicator.

I stop catty-corner and take a quick closer look, noting it also has the glass T-top and showcases the stock maroon paint color with traditional red pinstripe — a car with raceable potential, but nothing flashy.

Satisfied with the result of my sleuthing efforts so far, I return to the entrance side, position my bike in one of the available racks, unlock my chain, loop it around everything, and click it in place.

My gaze drifts up to the building as I adjust my purse. Based on the company logo, the word *crowbar* in the title is definitely a play on something mechanic and assures me this restaurant and bar caters to people who appreciate the road life. Motorcycles, to be precise; the wheel bracketed by angel wings is a dead giveaway.

A theme after this girl's own heart.

CHAPTER FIVE

When the door chimes this late into my shift, chances are the customer has their sights set on the bar, so I always try to make it a point to holler a greeting at newcomers from my side of the counter. This time is no different. The bell chimes, and I don't even bother to look up before yelling, "Welcome to The Crowbar!"

The grill closes in about five minutes. If they're not here for drinks, the door will chime again in three… two… one…

No chime.

Swiping over the mess my last customer made, I put on my best money-making smile and lift my attention toward the entrance, seeking out my next tip.

A hot college-aged woman with fucking legs for days and shorts that show 'em off and then some is not what I expect to see. My hand stops cleaning mid-action for a split second before returning to the task as her eyes find mine and she begins approaching the bar.

"Welcome to the Crowbar," I greet, idiot-grin still plastered on my face. Her focus drops to the unique motorcycle-style barstools we're famous for.

"You said that already," she chuckles, running her hand over the curved seat. "I've never seen seats like this at a bar."

"Yeah… they're fake motorcycles."

Well, duh. Classy, man. The fuck is wrong with you?

Even more amused now, her earlier chuckle turns into a laugh. "Yeah, I gathered as much." She winks at me and my brain misfires, shooting thoughts to my cock rather than helping me speak things like words.

Swallowing over the sudden tightness in my throat as she slings her leg over to mount the bike seat, I attempt speaking: "Umm… we… have…" She lifts her ass slightly in the air to adjust her positioning before settling, curving her fingers over the handlebars and twisting them in her grip.

"Have… what?" Her sultry voice has my eyes immediately redirecting from between her thighs back to… the spot on the counter that has now officially been scrubbed raw.

The second part of what I'd been trying to relay doesn't come out much better, but at least it finally comes out: "…regular stools on the other end… if you get uncomfortable."

"No way! This is great." Propping her feet onto the footpegs, she bounces a bit against the cushion, lifts her gaze, and flashes me a grin.

Returning with a smile of my own, I toss the rag into the sink, wash my hands, and ask, "Drinking tonight? What can I get for you?" Back in my customer-service element, I let the ordering process lead conversation from here, since I can't seem to communicate otherwise.

She takes in a deep breath and drums her fingers against the handlebar. "Surprise me?"

My lips turn up in a half-grin. "Sure thing. Gonna need to see some identification first, though."

She digs the card out of her purse, leans forward to compensate for the extra distance because of the fake gas tank, and slides her license across the counter. When I pluck up the card, my eyes immediately fall to her birthdate out of habit, but a spiking curiosity has me taking a quick peek at everything else, too.

Remi Delancey, twenty-three, black hair and brown eyes, five-eight, California address. *Too bad these damn things don't include a phone number.*

"California, hm?" I ask, handing her the card and stealing a quick brush of her fingers with mine when she accepts. "I'd ask where your friends are, but since the college summer break season ended about a month ago, I assume they're probably already back on the West Coast hitting the books." I pull several different liquors off the shelf and begin pouring them one by one into a tall, curvy glass.

"Just moved here with my brother and a friend of ours. Still getting situated. Figured I'd take a stroll around the area."

"By yourself? At ten-thirty at night?" I ask with the raise of an eyebrow as I add a splash of coke to top off her drink.

"Hey, I can hold my own," she defends. If she's offended by my poor choice of words, though, the smirk she pairs with the comment covers any possible frustration. I swipe a napkin off the pile, put it down in front of her, and place the drink on top.

She immediately picks it up, pinches the small straw between her fingers, gives it a swirl, and takes a sip. "W-wow…" Wetness gathers in her eyes, and she blinks fast. "A… Long Island. This is a 'get her drunk and take her home' kinda drink. We doing something tonight I don't know about yet?"

That stops me dead in my tracks. Thanks to the smooth direction our conversation had taken, helping to tame the initial shock of her nut-busting presence, I'm able to continue shootin' the shit as per my usual. Leaning my elbows on the bar in front of her and clasping my hands together, I respond with a half-cocked confidence. "Hmm, I don't know… are we?"

Remi places her drink between us and leans forward, driver-in-motion style, on the bike seat. "Hmm, I don't even know your na—"

"Trenton."

31

Whoa there. Let up a bit on the gas, man.

She laughs, straightens, picks up her drink again, and glances to each side of the bar. Skipping the straw this time, she lifts the glass to her mouth and takes a big swallow. "Not very busy right now, I see. Does that mean you'll be getting off soon?"

Getting off—

Damn, I wish I could say yes.

Instead, I match her distance by removing my elbows from the counter and try hard not to continue steering the conversation in a perverted way. "It'll pick up here in a few minutes. Usually does around this time on a Friday night."

"So… Trenton. Do you go by Trent for short?"

"Nope. I prefer Trenton. Or T-Top… for those who get close."

She takes another sip, lifting an eyebrow up at me from behind the rim of her drink before balancing the glass on the curved bump of the seat. "Does that mean the Monte Carlo outside belongs to you?"

Fuuuuck me.

This woman.

Surprising myself, I manage to conjure up a witty response in record time despite the building pressure. "Depends… are you the *domestic* type?"

"Well now, we've already concluded that I'm an import kinda gal," she tosses back, once again shocking me senseless.

I inch closer to the counter, both to hide my growing… attraction… and to get closer to the woman causing it. Which, of course, doesn't help at all with the *growing* part. Pretending horror at the import reference, I place my hand over my chest and gasp. "Mm, such a shame. Better make you a water to chase that Long Island."

CHAPTER SIX

A real laugh erupts from deep in my belly — the type of laugh I'd been convinced would take a miracle to pull from me again anytime soon. However, Trenton doesn't give me water; instead, he presents me with another Long Island, throwing away the first napkin and centering the new glass on a fresh one. "On the house," he says with a wink.

Mine or yours? is how I'm tempted to respond, feeling more and more alcohol-confident by the second. But I manage to rein it in, reminding myself that I'm not here to make friends — or anything else of the sort — no matter how much of an amazing first impression he made.

Trenton leans back against the far counter, shoving his rag-covered fist into a clean, wet glass, sepia-colored eyes watching and waiting for me to take the first taste of his next concoction and approve. Humoring him, I place my now-empty glass beside the new one and make the swap.

Just as I'm slipping the straw between my lips, the entrance door chimes, and his attention darts over

34

my head toward the activity. This time, he doesn't yell the greeting like he had when I arrived, though.

Instead, recognition sparks in his light-brown eyes as they track the movement of whoever had entered. Trenton steps forward, pats the bar in front of me, drops his gaze to mine for a couple heartbeats and says, "Make sure you don't go anywhere before I can get your number."

I shrug one of my shoulders and give him half-grin while sipping more of the drink. He gives me a playful groan in return but leaves nonetheless, taking off toward the far end of the bar.

"Crow! My man!" Trenton's voice travels the length of the counter and meets my ears. The sip I had begun to take stops mid-way up the straw, and my eyes spring open.

Crow?

As nonchalantly as possible, I ease my gaze in their direction. Trenton reaches his arm out, and the two men clasp hands. This guy — Crow — is all tattoos, piercings, and black clothing. The very picture of the type I usually go home with. Even though I was seriously considering Trenton's playful proposal a bit ago despite him being quite the opposite in appearance — and personality if I had to wager a guess.

Crow's teeth toy with the labret piercing in the center of his bottom lip as he slides an envelope across the counter. To add kindling to my now-simmering insides, the hand he does so with has a tattoo on each knuckle.

Trenton folds and pockets the envelope, and Crow leans over the counter, getting close and speaking something just low enough that I am unable to make out what is being said.

Before these damn Long Islands get me into any trouble, I decide my sleuthing efforts have unearthed enough information for one night; I decoded a possible meetup location and met at least one car enthusiast. As a hopeful next-step measure, I swipe a napkin off the pile, dig a pen and some cash out of my purse, jot down my name and number, and shove it into the tip jar along with a twenty-dollar bill. Then, I hop off the bike seat and slip out before Trenton catches me sneaking away.

* * *

THE DOOR CHIMES when opened. In a minor panic, I dart a glance over my shoulder before slipping out and pulling the door closed. The quick inspection proved Trenton was too immersed in his conversation with Crow to bother with the sound of the door giving away my hasty exit.

Unfortunately, my luck ends there as I run smack-dab into someone taking the corner right by the entrance. To make matters worse, I'm still close enough to the door that I bounce off the guy, and my back presses against the door handle, causing his chest… and things… to pin me on the spot.

Just as shocked as I am, he promptly staggers backward. My hand darts up to my chest in order to keep my heart from breaking past my ribcage. "Oh… shit… sorry," he stutters, clearly trying to pull himself together just as much as I am.

Blinking repeatedly, I take several recovery breaths before stepping aside and apologizing myself. "I was distracted coming out; it's my fault." Now that the initial surprise encounter has worn off, I am able to get a better look. The guy seems to be about my age but the glasses he's wearing make him look a bit younger, so I'm not entirely sure.

My gaze moves from his face to his choice of attire — a black shirt that says, "Select your ship:" and showcases several popular vehicles from various different science fiction movies and shows.

With a grin, I simply state, "Why choose?" The guy pushes up his glasses with a knuckle and shifts from foot to foot. "Your shirt? If they're all available, might as well take 'em each for a spin, right?"

He darts a glance down at his shirt as though he'd forgotten which one he tossed on tonight. "Oh. Heh. Right." One awkward chuckle later, his eyes finally meet mine.

The awkwardness doesn't quite go away as I had hoped, though. I pipe up, "Okay… well… ah… on that note, I'm gonna just hop on my high-tech bicycle over here and be on my way," as I slowly walk backward toward the rack.

The guy dips his head, shoves a hand into his pocket, and swiftly enters the building without a second glance. I spin on my heels toward the bike rack and hurry to pop the lock. But I don't leave the place right away — not without first doing one more loop around the parking lot. Trenton was right, the place is picking up. More cars fill spaces which might just mean more evidence to back up my sleuthing efforts. Plus, call me curious, but I'm dying to know what Crow drives — even if it means taking a wild guess.

Just as I'm heading toward the back, a new vehicle enters: a third-gen Trans Am. The corner of my lips tick upward, and I continue my route. Sure enough, parked right beside Trenton's Monte Carlo is a black Supra. Beside the Supra… a… well, a car with the body style of a Bimmer — maybe an E30? — but clearly modified, so I might not quite have the model nailed.

Assessment complete, I'd bet my bottom dollar that the black Supra belongs to the one and only Crow.

If the tires are any indication, I've definitely found something; regular tires don't have grips like the ones this has.

These cars practically have "car club" written all over them even despite no glaringly obvious decals giving it away.

CHAPTER SEVEN

Crow

"**G**oddammit, Crow. You scared her away with all that ink and broodiness you carry around everywhere you go." Trenton squints at a spot above me, and his eyes unfocus as he whispers, "Tilting my head just right, I can almost see the hovering, dark cloud."

Humoring him with a comeback takes too much effort, so I stick with playing on that so-called broodiness just to fuck with him more. "Who?" I ask.

Trenton glares at me, shaking his head, as he pours a smooth golden stream of liquor over a glass filled with ice cubes.

"Dark hair, dark-brown eyes, fuck-me-now legs?" A familiar voice meets my ears just before the empty barstool beside me screeches against the hardwood floor, pulling my attention away from my soon-to-be liquid escape. Hayes slips onto the seat and scoots it forward.

"Yep, that's the one. She started throwing out words like 'domestic' and 'import'. Think I might make her my wife one day." Trenton flashes Hayes a grin, grabs another glass from the back counter, and tosses a few ice cubes inside, turning my order into a double.

"Wife? Is this our new code word for bed warmer?" Hayes huffs out a laugh. I remove his earnings from my pocket and hand the envelope over.

"See" — Trenton slides the two of us our Bourbons on ice — "even Hayes noticed her. What the fuck is wrong with you, Crow?"

"Yeah, I bumped into her as she was leaving. Guess she's not from around here?" Hayes asks. We all grew up in Bay County, and between the three of us, we know most of the people who visit The Crowbar — or get to know them pretty quick.

During tourist seasons, everyone is a new face. The rest of the year, if someone like her walks into the bar, locals are bound to notice.

"Cali girl. Just moved here with her brother and a friend. Did you catch what she was driving?" Trenton asks, all ears as he restocks the straws.

"Not exactly, no. She was headed toward the bike rack, though. Asked me about my shirt. Seemed... nice."

"Yeah, well no thanks to *Burke* here, she was about five more swallows away from being a whole hell of a lot nicer." Trenton tosses out my birth name like he has business doing so. Fucker is damn lucky I like him. If anyone else calls me that, we'll have problems.

41

Did I miss the hot piece of ass sitting on the motorcycle stool? No. I definitely saw her. Pretty sure everyone in this building did. The fact that Trenton "T-Top" Stokes missed his chance makes my night, though; I can count on one hand how many times a woman has turned him down.

"Sounds like you're losing your edge, T-Top." The chuff of my laugh causes a cloud of condensation to stream out of my drink as I lift the cool glass to my mouth and throw the liquid back in one shot.

Trenton raises an eyebrow at me as he backs away toward where she'd been sitting. After wiping down the counter and tossing the dirty napkins into a trash bin, he picks up the tip jar and returns to our side of the bar. Like a good friend, he grabs the Bourbon and pours more into my glass before dumping out the jar's contents.

Hayes takes a single swig of his drink and puts it down, cupping the glass between both hands.

"My cock hasn't softened since she asked if the Monte Carlo outside was mine." To elaborate this point, Trenton cups and jostles himself.

"You... have a serious problem," I state. The man is a damn fiend. With another single gulp, I finish the second glass quicker than the first.

"Damn straight I do." He turns the tip jar over and gives it a good shake. "She's not getting in my bed tonight. That's a real big prob—" Trenton peers into the tip jar, reaches his hand inside, and pulls out a napkin that had gotten stuck.

He takes hold of it, fingers pinching the corners at ten-and-two, eyes scanning something Hayes and I can't see from this angle. The damp ink that bled through the back gives us a pretty damn good idea, though.

Trenton flips the napkin around, smiling like an idiot. "Guess you weren't scary enough," he says with all the smugness in the world as he pulls out his phone.

"Come on… Right now? Really?" I reach forward to snatch the phone from his hand, but the two — going on three — Bourbons are no match for his quick reflexes. "At least make her sweat it out a bit. You know, play hard to get. Chicks dig that shit."

"Nah, man, that's your thing. I fucking see something I want and go for it." Thinking, he bites at the inside of his cheek, eyes still riveted on her phone number.

"Or… try getting awkward and cutesy like Hayes here," I advise.

Hayes chokes and sputters. "A-awkward and cutesy?"

"How did 'bumping' into her go?" I ask, screwing with him.

"It went fine." He grabs a napkin from over the counter and wipes the Bourbon off his chin.

"Haaaayes, Hayes, Hayes" — I pinch his cheek — "your ears are turning red."

He jerks his face away, reaches over, and slaps me upside the head. "She took me by surprise, smartass. I might be shit at talking to girls, but they don't really seem to mind when I'm balls deep and all they can do is scream, '*Oh yes, oh yes, oh yes*,' anyway."

Trenton finally looks up from the napkin. "Hayes is a fucking beast. He does all that romantic stuff and shit; warms 'em up nice. Makes my part a piece of cake."

"Oh, and what is your part?" The fact that these two tag team is not lost on me. They like to share. Always have.

Fucking psychos.

"The most important part, of course."

My eyebrows lift.

With a side-smirk, Hayes finishes the comment Trenton had started. "Convincing them that two's company." Nursing another sip and finishing off his point by gesturing toward the phone Trenton is now thumbing a text into, he adds, "Trenton takes care of the talking part."

"Two Bourbons in… I assume we're not racing tonight?" Trenton asks, studying the screen intently.

"Three," I correct, sliding my glass across the bar. "But, yeah. Just hanging out and spreading the word."

"Signed, sealed, and delivered." He beams, folding the napkin neatly, pressing it to the back of his phone, and tucking them securely into his back pocket.

The entrance door dings, and I check my watch. Newbie, no doubt; the long-time club members don't bother showing until the lot starts to fill.

Hayes leans to the side, slips a rubber-banded stack of "golden" tickets from his jeans, and slides them across the counter to Trenton. Trenton snatches them up, removes the envelope I'd given him, and opens it up to place the tickets inside. With a low whistle, he fingers through the bills before plucking a single ticket from the stack, adding the rest to the envelope, and shoving it under the counter for easy access.

A young guy, barely an adult if I had to guess, heads straight toward the bar, and Trenton yells out his usual, "Welcome to The Crowbar!" before stepping sideways to the section of the counter it looks like the guy is approaching. "Sup, man. Grill is closed, but the bar is open until two. Can I get you something to drink?"

The guy raps his fingers on the bar top. "Um…" His glassy eyes roll up toward the ceiling.

"09040139," he recites the forum post timestamp, squinting.

One number off.

Trenton gives the kid a good once-over before sliding the ticket across the counter.

"You hanging out for a while?" Trenton asks as the guy reads the details and shoves the small paper into his pocket.

"Sure," he responds, extending a hand. "Name's Boyd."

"Nice to meet you, Boyd. Welcome to the club."

CHAPTER EIGHT

Remi

Thankfully, Trenton made that second drink weaker than the first. Last thing I need right now is a DUI or a charge of "reckless driving" while on my bicycle.

Nevertheless, I still feel pretty warm and light, so I take a backroad that runs parallel to the main street. After experiencing the lack of bicycle-friendly lanes and sidewalks, I just might take this route from here on out seeing as it leads all the way home.

What's worse than the city's poor transportation infrastructure, however, is the fact I can't get a certain bartender out of my mind — haven't been able to since walking out the door. A combination of giddiness and tentative anticipation swims in my belly right along with the mix of liquors.

For the briefest of moments, I considered waiting around to swap phone numbers with him, but I didn't want to come across as too obvious should he be one of the guys involved in the club Jude and Porter are looking for.

Now, the ball is in his court, and I'm left wondering if he really intended on using my phone number or if he was just saying that to... I don't know... impress me or get a bigger tip, I guess.

Images of Crow flick through my mind, too, since the small amount of information I've uncovered seems to point directly at him — the crow avatar, meeting at the Crowbar, the parked Supra. Of the three vehicles I pegged as car club types, that sporty Supra is the most likely candidate for racing.

I twist my handlebars left and right, swerving into a curvy zigzag at the thought of turning around and rubbing shoulders with the brooding, tattooed man just to see how much more information I can glean.

But since something small has already been established with Trenton, he might be the easier trail to follow. Those dark, pensive types are often high maintenance. They put up too much of a chase and have too many barely-functioning spare parts and not enough trust-worty original pieces. Or something.

Whatever the appropriate analogy, the fact that little nugget is precisely why I am such a damn whore for them is besides the point.

Balancing hands-free, I swat at the air, waving away the thought.

There's always a chance these guys are just part of a regular car club and have nothing to do with the underground racing scene. Car clubs are a dime a dozen in beach areas like these, ranging from predominantly high school-aged groups on up into middle-aged classics fanatics.

Illegal street racing, though? That's typically reserved for the young and stupid. Old enough to drive; young enough to still believe they are invincible.

A stop sign halts my thoughts right along with my bike as I screech to a stop. My eyes seek out my new home just ahead as I pedal through the four-way.

From here, everything appears dark upstairs. Hopefully, I'll be able to slip in unnoticed.

I turn into the driveway, cruise under the deck, park my bicycle, and pop the kickstand before taking the stairs two at a time to the top level and quietly sliding the glass door open.

Porter and Jude claimed the entire downstairs because of the pool table and wet bar. Me, on the other hand? The second floor with the kitchen, fireplace, and office is my domain.

This arrangement gives me some peace and quiet in the mornings and evenings. Tonight is a perfect example as both Jude and Porter appear to be either asleep or downstairs watching television.

I hurry down the hallway to where it dead ends at my bedroom. Feeling the buzz of liquor and endorphins from bicycling, I throw myself onto the bed, tossing my purse onto the side table mid-launch.

Not even two seconds after my head hits the pillow, my phone chimes, indicating a new text.

Rolling sideways, I scramble to the table. After fumbling with the zipper for a time, the phone is in my hand and I return to lying on my back, cocooning myself in the feathertop mattress.

:Unknown Number: Hey, a twenty must've fallen from your purse when you tackled my friend outside of The Crowbar. Guess he decided to shove it in my tip jar for safe keeping. What's your address? We'll swing by on our way home to drop it off.

My upper teeth press down on my bottom lip to control the giddy smile that tries inching up. Ah, so the awkward cutie I bumped into was a friend of his...

:Me: Oh... the one who drives a Bimmer? Wears glasses? Super cute?

Still curious if the Supra does indeed belong to Crow, I cast a line regarding which of the cars parked near the Monte Carlo is owned by the guy I bumped into.

While waiting for a response, I quickly add Trenton as a contact before I forget.

:Trenton: *Yep, that guy. Feels terrible about the mishap and has been drinking away his feelings since he got here. I kinda promised him I would make sure you're taken care of. Wouldn't want to let him down, you know?*

Just the fact that he texted me at all has heat coiling low inside me. I know how these things work — back and forth texts like this between two interested adults. The thought alone has my nerves buzzing. There's no way he can come here, though. Jude and Porter would have a field day giving him a hard time.

I love my brother, but he's definitely protective. Especially since Dad died.

As for Porter… yeah… no.

Recipe for disaster.

:Me: *You're a good friend, Trenton. He is a lucky guy. Let him know the drinks are on me… since he found my twenty. Finders keepers and all.*

The flashing dots indicate he's typing a response before my text even shows as delivered.

:Trenton: *I'm going to take a major leap here and be candid as hell…*

More flashing dots.

51

:Trenton: Truth is, I haven't been able to get you out of my mind since you walked into the bar. Not knowing if I'm going to see you again is slowly killing me inside.

At that, a snort-laugh bursts out of me.

:Me: You just want to get into my pants.

:Trenton: You were wearing shorts, but if you're speaking figuratively, then yes… that is correct. But not "just" your pants. I meant it when I said that I haven't been able to get you off my mind.

I start and restart a response at least a dozen times before deciding what to go with. A small dagger pierces my heart and I deflate a little — this puts me in quite the predicament. If I turn him down, I might lose my contact. If I take him up on the offer — which is what I'd really like to do — I might find myself in deeper than I want to be.

There's a fine line, and I'm not quite sure how to walk it.

:Me: The feeling is mutual…

I go ahead and send that part through, intending on making it a two-part response, but a rap on my door startles me out of the thought process.

For years, Jude has been in the habit of not being able to fall asleep when I go out. Remedied only when I arrive home safely. We might be grown adults, but that man would rope the moon for me. I will forever be his *baby* sister.

I pad over to the door and open it. Rather than Jude's dark-brown eyes meeting mine, Porter leans against the hallway wall. The smell of stale beer wafts toward me when he nudges the door open the rest of the way with his foot.

The phone in my hands turns into lead as I curve my arms behind my back to hide the conversation between Trenton and me. With shaky fingers, I locate the volume control and hold the down button until it softly vibrates.

Porter pushes off the wall and walks forward. I stumble backward, not expecting the sudden approach. Once he's completely inside my room, his hand darts out behind him and he slams the door shut, the unmistakable click of the door lock engaging soon follows.

"Hey… w-what's up?"

Silly Remi… you know he isn't here for casual conversation.

The teenage girl inside me remembers these signs all too well, while the grown woman still foolishly tries to pretend otherwise.

Porter continues forward, and I move backward in sync until the back of my knees hit the bed and I can't go any farther.

"You are," he says, leaning forward. "Usually you're asleep by now." My ass lands on the bed with a bounce. As soon as my hands meet the cool sheets, I slip my phone under the pillow. "Something I need to know about what kept you out so late?" he presses.

He… he was here when I left. He knows how late it was already. Fearing I might give him the wrong answer, my mind reels with attempts to decode the meaning behind his words — to come up with the response he wants to hear so that maybe tonight will be my lucky night and he will turn right back around and leave just as quickly as he came.

Porter has never been fond of me going out, especially where other guys are concerned. Up until we moved here, though, our home lives were separate. It was a rare occurrence that my relationships crossed paths with his involvement in the family business or friendship with Jude.

Is that what this is all about? The potential of me becoming involved with someone other than him? Or is it simply that he's chomping at the bit to get any information about my visit to The Crowbar?

"Not sure I love this silence, Remi." Porter pushes his hand through my hair until all the long strands are gathered in his fist at my nape. He wrenches my head back so that my attention jerks up toward his face rather than being in line with the bulge behind the zipper of his jeans.

Perhaps I should share every little detail about the guys I met and their cars, but something inside me rebels. Even as tears prick at my eyes from the sting of his grip, I shake my head in response to the question.

One visit — one conversation — is hardly enough.

There's nothing to be said about me being out late.

At least that's the lie I'm telling myself.

Maybe it'll be enough to convince him, too.

I angle to the side, hoping he will let me go. When his fingers loosen, relief leaves my body on a pathetic exhale. A fleeting moment later, my muscles tense again as he drops into a squat and presses his palms against my thighs, pinning me in place. "You wouldn't keep information from me, would you?" The words come in a mere whisper as Porter drapes our shared secrets over me like a sopping-wet towel.

"A decent ride in employee parking," I choke out, giving in to his manipulative threats far too easily. "Nothing more. Pretty sure the owner was on the clock. I'll continue looking in the morning after some sleep."

When his nose trails a line from beneath my ear, over my jaw, and to my cheek, the scent of alcohol hits me hard. "Just once more," he whispers, breathing me in. "Like old times."

"You're drunk," I squeak.

"Never stopped you before."

Before, as in when I was young, naive, and smitten.

Before, when he would weave his promises and paint beautiful pictures so flawlessly.

Before, when I was still innocent.

"Fuck you, Porter."

"Well… thanks for the consent, because that's exactly what you're going to do."

CHAPTER NINE

J ude eventually checks on me — after Porter leaves, my long and hot shower is complete, tears are dried, and a cool pillow is under my head.

I wasn't asleep — I couldn't sleep — but I pretended to be anyway. Since, as I have discovered, I'm so damn good at that these days. Pretending.

The door opens and closes, and as soon as the latch clicks, I inch the covers down from where they'd been tucked up near my chin to past my shoulders.

This isn't the first time Porter has gotten carried away, especially when he feels challenged. I allow it, because refusing gives him full control. By consenting, at least then the control is mine... in a sick and twisted sort of way.

But even the hot shower and the millions of tears that tried to wash away the sting of his knuckles against my cheek doesn't clean away the feel of him off — and out — of me.

His touch, his breath, his wet mouth... all of it lingers and crawls along every inch of my skin.

I flip over and slip my hand under the pillow in an attempt to get comfortable. My forgotten phone bumps my fingertips, and I wrap them around the plastic case with a sigh. Thoughts of Trenton, Crow, and the guy who owns the Bimmer return to the forefront of my mind.

Right now, those guys might very well be my saving grace, and the link to everything I need to know. Trenton made it quite clear what his intentions were. Where his sights were aimed. My potential "in" just became that much easier.

Eventually, my curiosity as to whether or not he continued texting after I had left him hanging has me unburying the phone and flipping onto my back. The bright light webs over my face as I scan the notifications.

:Trenton: Why do I feel like there's a "but" coming?

He had replied to my previous open-ended response but didn't send anything else — didn't press further.

I tap the side of my phone, teeth digging into my bottom lip. Tonight's escapades with Porter has my nerves on edge and mind reeling with too many thoughts to get any amount of sleep.

My chest tightens and stomach rolls as I contemplate the idea of re-opening the topic of spending a night with Trenton.

Emphasis on "A."

One night.

Tonight.

Just so I don't have to spend another second sleeping in the bed Porter was just in with me. To feel something — someone — on my body other than him.

And maybe, just maybe, so I can get the damn information needed to get Porter off my back.

Then, perhaps the money promised to me when successful will be enough to put a down payment on my own place.

:Me: Pssst... are you still awake? Sorry for the late text, but something unexpected came up and I got pulled away.

:Trenton: Hey, yeah. I'm still at the bar. We don't close until 2.

I check the time.
1:37 a.m.

:Me: You were right. There's a "but."

Again, I leave him hanging while I run through ways to make this happen in my mind.

:Me: But... meeting at my place isn't going to work, so how about yours instead? There's also a caveat.

:Trenton: Oooh, tell me more. And, yes, my place works.

:Me: I'm going to need a ride…

:Trenton: Oh, I'll give you a ride. ;) But also, I'll give you a ride. Both types of rides. Where can I pick you up?

:Me: Um… behind the Regency hotel?

:Trenton: You want me to pick you up on the beach in the middle of the night? That's shady as hell… are you going to take advantage of me?

My stomach twists at the thought. Because I am… that's exactly what I'm going to do. But he's doing the same with me, right?

:Me: That's the plan. But also, there's a small public parking area there, so I figured it'd be an easy in and out.

:Trenton: Heh. That's what she said.

:Me: Haha. Clever. When can I expect to see you?

:Trenton: Every day for the rest of our lives… *Starting at 2:15?*

:Me: Now you're the one being shady… Are you going to steal me and keep me as your pet?

:Trenton: There's an idea…

:Me: See you soon… I'll bring the leash.

:Trenton: Mmm damn. This is going to be the longest end of shift of my life. See you in thirty.

I don't bother to respond, because I have a feeling that the two of us could just keep going forever. Talking to him in the bar was easy, and our texting conversation flows naturally.

Plus, I need to change out of my pajamas and figure out a way to sneak out of here as soon as possible or I won't make it to the rendezvous spot in time.

I never in a million years would have imagined myself as a grown-ass woman sneaking out of my bedroom to hang out with a cute guy. But desperate times call for desperate measures.

I open the window and peer outside. Thankfully, just below my room there's a small shed that butts up against the wooden privacy fence. By exiting this way, I can keep my bedroom door locked so Jude and Porter won't come barging in and find me gone. Meeting at the Regency means I can leave my bike here and walk the short couple of blocks.

I pad over to my closet and rake my eyes over the many options. Ready to cut ties before they're too firmly knotted, I decide to go full throttle and wear one of my car shirts after all. The "Race Like a Girl" one definitely does the trick. Too flashy? Maybe. But I want to be over with this ploy as fast as possible.

Racing shirt, black distressed jeans, Converses — triple check. My hair had begun to dry naturally and has a small wave going, so I decide to keep it down and let the gulf breeze take care of the rest while waiting for Trenton to show up.

Purse settled across my body and hanging at my hip, I climb out the window, jump down onto the rooftop, and scale the wooden fence until my feet meet sandy ground.

To get to the front of the house, though, I have to walk past the floor-to-ceiling windows that sprawl across the bottom floor. Since the sun rises and sets on the sides of the house, Jude and Porter have decided not to bother with hanging shades or curtains. Thankfully, I have the cover of night at my disposal… and my signature black clothes to boot.

Rather than dart across the backyard right in front of the windows, I stick to slinking along the perimeter of the fence instead.

By the time I'm rounding the corner toward the front of the house, sandspurs are twisted in my laces and sand has sunk inside my shoes. But I manage to escape without any problems otherwise, and that's what matters.

The rest is a piece of cake.

CHAPTER TEN

At two in the morning the beach is empty. Miles of shore and dunes can be seen both left and right. The gulf is a blanket of black straight ahead, with the reflection of balcony lights from the high-rise condo behind me shimmering on the surface.

There is a light breeze but ever present nonetheless as it tends to be in areas like this. The waves break in quiet whooshes on the shore, and the wind whistles lightly in my ears. I close my eyes and, for a moment, am back home in California.

Unlike the beige sand in Cali, the sand here is fluffy and white. Snow like, minus the cold. Beautiful.

With a deep inhale and exhale of the salty breeze, I let my mind believe for a moment that all is well with the world. That I am just a girl on the beach — just an average drop of water in an ocean of others.

Not the daughter of the infamous and recently deceased Troy Delancey.

Not the sister of the man following in Daddy's footsteps.

Not the plaything of a guy bent on making my life a living hell.

Just Remi Delancey.

"Remi?" A voice raises over the sounds of the beach surrounding me. My eyes spring open, and I push off the sandy ground, dusting my hands off as I turn to face the direction from which it came.

Trenton is tromping through the thick sand barefoot with his jeans rolled up at the bottom. He, too, is wearing a black shirt with white lettering. Only when we are just a few feet from each other am I able to read it: "If it isn't fast, I'm not interested."

I press my lips together to hide the stupid grin trying to give away my amusement. At The Crowbar he was wearing a polo shirt with a logo on the pocket.

Trenton had been reading the wording on my top at the same time. Letting out a chuckle, he doesn't bother to hide his mirth. "My friend said you came to The Crowbar on a bike. You race on a bike?"

"Yes, of course. I'll race on just about anything with wheels: skates, boards, bikes."

Throwing his arm around my shoulders, he turns us around so we can leave the beach and head toward his car.

Since he had no trouble bringing up my shirt, I follow his lead: "So... about yours. We talking cars or women?"

Trenton snorts. "Both."

His confidence and straight-forward approach are quite refreshing. There's nothing manipulative there, nothing sleazy. He wants to fuck, and he's not hiding that behind poor attempts to feign interest beyond anything other than that simple, primal desire.

While I like flowers and dinner dates like the rest of 'em, sometimes this works, too — two consenting adults out to have a good time for a few hours.

Do I think this makes me less respectable? No.

Am I worried he might think such a thing? Again, no.

Of course, there's always the fact that I am also following through with this because I need information.

But the rest — the fun part that will happen behind closed doors tonight? That part is for me.

A big middle finger to Porter, and a warm hug and a pat on the back for myself. Because I mean, damn, considering the shitstorm my life has been over the past few months, I could use a little fun.

When we get to the small path that leads to public parking, Trenton removes his arm from my shoulders and picks up the black work shoes he had placed on the edge of the walkway. We continue forward, and I sit down on the top step and begin taking off my shoes.

I know how this works with car guys. Well, some types. I haven't quite pegged Trenton as the sort that will flip out if someone gets inside his car without either taking their shoes off first or at least making sure there's nothing in or on them that will dirty up the floorboard.

Since my shoes are a hot mess right now, I go ahead and remove them, slip each shoe through the opening in the railing along the walkway, and dump the sand out. Then, I situate the shoes in my lap and begin prying off each sandspur.

Trenton watches me intently as he dusts the sand off the bottoms of his feet and proceeds to put his socks and shoes back on. Once done, he sits beside me, takes the shoe I'm not working on, and places it in his own lap to help. "Damn," he says. "Were you swimming in the dunes or something?"

With a grin and shake of my head, I explain, "Ah, not quite. We haven't had time to take care of any landscaping at our new place yet; our yard is riddled with them."

Trenton nods, side-eyeing me. "What happened to your cheek?" he asks on a whisper.

The comment catches me 100 percent off guard, and my hand comes up to the side of my face to cover the shiner Porter left behind. With a halfhearted chuckle, a lie falls from my lips far too easily: "Ate the pavement on my way home, no thanks to the couple of Long Islands some hot bartender at The Crowbar gave me."

Trenton's mouth pulls up at the side, and his gaze drops back to the task at hand. The two of us stay quiet as we finish clearing my laces. With a final swipe at the bottom of my feet, I slip the Converses back on and take Trenton's extended hand, allowing him to help me up.

His fingertips graze my palm as he slowly lets go, and his eyes alight on the red and slightly swollen mark on my face again. I try not to flinch or drop my gaze at the scrutiny.

The thought of covering it up never once crossed my mind since I seldom wear makeup anyway. Plus, it has been a few years since Porter has lashed out. Tonight, he just had too much to drink is all.

One thing is for certain: if I act the damsel or drop my gaze, it will look a lot more like a bicycle incident had nothing to do with it.

"You look different then you did at the bar," he says, dragging his thumb over the delicate spot.

My belly does a painful flip. "Better? Worse?" I want to drop my gaze for entirely other reasons now because the look he's giving me is not a secured one-night stand look. It is the look of something more…

"There isn't anything better," he returns, focus finally leaving the mark and dropping to my mouth.

Why is he doing this? He already knows I'm going to sleep with him. "Trenton…"

"Hmm?" His eyes dart back up to mine.

"The flowers are beautiful and all, but now that you've handed them to me, I think it's time to put them in a vase." The words come out whispery as my own gaze finally drops down to his mouth and beyond to the bob of his throat as he works out the analogy.

"Oh… right." After a couple blinks, he flashes me a big grin. "Wanna go for a ride?"

My eyes flick beyond him to the only car parked in the lot before returning. "Yeah, I would."

CHAPTER ELEVEN

When I prop my feet on the side sill and look over my shoulder, eyebrow raised, he laughs. "Damn girl, where have you been all my life?" he says, ending it with the press of his teeth against his bottom lip. Clearing his throat, he gives me a brief head tilt to indicate that he doesn't mind if my shoes are on or off.

I let out a mental sigh of relief and, before making my entrance official and placing my purse beside my feet on the floorboard, give them one more good kick together as an added measure to make sure there isn't any lingering sand stuck to the bottoms.

Despite the outside being all stock, the inside of his car is a major contrast. Everything… and I mean *everything* is custom — the seats, dashboard, gearshift, aftermarket gauges, interior lights. Everything. "A sleeper," I mumble to myself, raking my gaze over each little detail.

Eventually my eyes land on Trenton who is now blinking at me, hand frozen on his key in mid-startup. "There is about a half of a single percent of the entire female population that actually knows the term 'sleeper' and what that even means."

Shit. Apparently I said that louder than I realized. Coughing into my fist, I try to recover the slip. If that's even what it was. Apparently I'm not as great at pretending after all. "Sleepers. Stock on the outside, heavy mods everywhere else." I give him a haughty wink. "Ex-boyfriend was — is — a car guy."

Oh, and my brother and Dad, too. Not to mention all the fingers we had dipped in the industry...

For now, I choose to stick with the basics, though.

Trenton turns the key over and she rumbles to life. All muscle and grit. I might be an import gal, but I can appreciate the older, domestic beasts like this. Chargers, Shelbys, GTOs. They're just a completely different class. They sound different, feel different, drive different...

And, yeah, they race differently, too.

"Oh? What did — does — he drive?"

My eyes immediately roll upward to the roof of his car which is actually not a roof at all but the glass of his T-top. "Mustang GT."

Trenton snort-laughs. "Of course. Explains why you know a thing or two about domestics, though."

"Yeah."

"His a sleeper, too?" he asks, turning out of the parking lot.

"Gosh no. New model, couple of customizations but stock otherwise."

Please don't ask further; I don't want to lie to you more than I already have.

71

Continuing my study of the interior, I press my palm against the dark, reddish-purple leather and slide it over the full bench seat until my fingers bump the side of his thigh.

Trenton's focus leaves the road for a heartbeat, falling to where my fingers had stopped their journey.

"I'm honestly not sure I have ever ridden in a vehicle with bench seating." The gearshift is behind the steering wheel instead of between the passenger and driver seat. The seat fills the entire width of the car, the wide body style making the bench long enough to lie down on.

Well, long enough for *me* to lie down on. My perusal travels from the top of Trenton's messy dark-blond hair down to his legs. Not short by any means but definitely tall enough that he wouldn't be able to stretch out completely.

"What type of riding are we talking about?" He flashes me a grin.

"Both." A small smile of my own creeps up along with the pace of my pulse. I continue to consider the size of the seat, picturing a number of ways to use it. The glint of a buckle in the very center catches my eye — a middle passenger seat belt.

Without a second thought, I reach down, unbuckle, scoot over so that Trenton and I are hip-to-hip, pull the lap belt over my hips, and clip it in.

Since the drive shaft runs down the middle of the car, there's a slight hump on the floor. My options are to either open my legs and place a foot on each side or prop them up on top of the small protrusion. Since the latter is more uncomfortable, I opt for the former, slipping my left foot down under Trenton's leg and the right one on the passenger floorboard near my purse.

Wiggling a bit to get comfortable, I finalize my assessment before speaking again. "I really like what you've done — very impressive."

From what can be determined without seeing under the hood, that is. But I wouldn't want the poor guy to faint before we get to have any fun, so I refrain from prying about any of those modifications.

"Thanks." He lets out a quiet laugh, veering onto the overpass that leads toward town.

I shrug and my arm rubs against his. "Just calling it like I see it."

As we go over the bridge separating the beach side of the county from the town side, he switches his driving hand from right to left and drops his now-free hand on my leg. The gesture is simple and clear.

My body has no trouble translating that touch, either; a throb immediately ignites between my legs.

That's one of the nice things about hookups like this; there's no wondering what's going to happen. No worry as to whether or not the other party is interested or where the connection will lead. A man touches you like that, and his intentions are obvious.

Returning the gesture with a silent response, I place my hand on top, spread my fingers between his, then push him toward the point of me that aches more and more the longer we drive. Once we get to my inner thigh, Trenton's hand tightens without any further encouragement from me.

"How far away is your house?" I intentionally whisper, letting my breath fan over his ear and neck.

"Too far," he groans, giving my thigh another squeeze before running his middle finger along the inner seam of my jeans. His other hand leaves the steering wheel for a split second as he flicks the blinker on and merges into a left turn lane.

The light doesn't keep us waiting long; it changes from red to green arrow just in time to keep him from having to come to a complete stop before rolling through the intersection.

Our hands stay intertwined while he once more flicks his blinker on, turns right, and almost immediately takes a side road, over a train track, and then another left, promptly swinging one more left and pulling up to the lifting automatic door of a garage.

Trenton's fingers drum on the steering wheel while he waits until the garage door is high enough for him to drive us inside.

"I thought you said it was far—"

He throws the car into park, and his mouth crashes into mine.

CHAPTER TWELVE

Trenton manages to get both seat belts undone and my leg straddled over his lap in a dizzyingly-quick amount of time.

With my center hovered over his erection and lower back pressed against the steering wheel, both his hands come up to my face to cup my cheeks, the thumb that falls against the bruise of my cheekbone subconsciously lighter than all the rest of his fingers and his palms even despite the intensity of our kiss.

Not that it would matter anyway; there are so many endorphins — so much heat — coursing through me I'm not sure I would mind if he were to apply pressure.

But there's something about the small, gentle effort he makes that turns me on even more. The gentleness amid our passion.

His hands don't remain on my face for long, though. They soon journey a path down my neck, over my breasts, rib cage, and hips, and around to my ass, where he grasps, filling his palms.

"Mmm," he groans, his mouth leaving mine and moving to my chin and down toward the collar of my shirt. "The jeans are amazing but a lot more difficult to get into than the shorts you had on earlier," he explains before taking a nip of my neck.

My fingers unwrap from the hair at the back of his head and move to the bottom hem of my shirt. I pull it over my head and toss it to the passenger floorboard. Only my front-access bra remains, the small, centered clip begging to be released.

Trenton pulls his head back slightly, gaze dropping from where he had been kissing my neck down to my lace-covered breasts. He removes a hand from my ass, lifts his finger to the dip between my collar bone, and traces a line over my cleavage. Once the tip of his finger reaches the clasp, his thumb joins in to pinch the plastic and slide it apart.

After the clasp pops free, he drags his fingertips over my shoulders, moving both hands to my bra straps and sliding each down until the thin material slips off the rest of the way. Reaching around between my back and the steering wheel, he hooks his finger around the back strap and pulls the bra completely free, discarding it to join my shirt.

All this time, not a word is spoken between us. Trenton's eyes alight on each newly revealed inch of my skin with every slow step. Now that my own hands are free, I rise for a moment, grab the bottom of his shirt, and lift it up and over his head.

The garage's interior lighting shines through his windshield, bathing him in a white glow. The shadows cast on account of his tint create the appearance of deep grooves and ridges in all the right places along his arms and torso.

As soon as our shirts are together on the floorboard, his gaze moves over each breast, down to my belly button, and beyond to the pesky jeans before traveling back up again.

His hands lift, and just when I expect him to cup my breasts, one falls on my hip and the other skates across the side of my neck en route to the back of my head. He draws me toward him, bringing my breasts flush against his warm skin, and kisses me nice and slow. His dark-blond eyelashes drop down as his eyes close. The shadowy light casts long, spidery lines over his cheekbones. My own eyes soon follow, and I clasp my hands around his neck again.

Instead of waiting for him to deepen the kiss, I take control and tease his lips with the tip of my tongue. However, there's no challenge. Trenton matches me step for step, his tongue accepting the offer immediately and wrapping around mine while he drifts his hands to my ribcage.

With a slight bit of pressure from his left hand, he encourages me to lean toward the passenger seat. The two of us break apart, and he guides me to my back. I scoot backward until his fingers dig into my side halting my movement. Trenton reaches past me, pops his glove box, and pulls out a wrapped condom, quickly shoving it into his front pocket.

His fingers then graze over my stomach. The muscles flutter in response, and a side-smile pulls at his lips as those same fingers dip beneath the waistband of my jeans, skillfully pop the button, and open the zipper.

In this position, I am unable to do anything to help. Instead, I am at the mercy of his pacing.

And, despite what his now-discarded shirt says, Trenton takes his time.

His eyes soak me in.

His skin absorbs all my heat.

His fingertips read every single goosebump that rises beneath his touch.

When he's ready to take things a step further, he presses into the sides of my jeans and under my panties and I lift my hips to aid him in pulling the tight material and underwear down toward my ankles.

I am most certainly regretting my clothing choice. With this man? I should have just worn a skirt. Just the skirt. Nothing else. Problem is… I don't even own a skirt. Not a single one.

Peeling the jeans off takes a bit of effort, but Trenton is patient. And he never stops watching; his gaze burns a line on my skin from hip to ankle as he carefully removes every last inch of remaining material. When my feet need to come through, I draw my knees toward my stomach and wiggle my feet.

Finally free from restrictive clothing, I place one foot on the steering wheel, and the other toward the crease of the seat. Trenton looks at the roof of his car and rumbles out a groan before returning his gaze to mine and throwing me a wink.

A shaky, somewhat nervous chuckle trickles out of me. Completely bare to him, my heart pounds. It's beating so hard and fast, I'm certain he can see and measure each pulse as my breasts rise and fall, each breath nearly matching in intensity.

"You're gorgeous," he says, making my pulse thrum harder.

"You're just trying to get in—" I start to say the same quip I had jested about in our texts, but he places his hands on either side of my head and presses in close to me, jeans rubbing between my bare thighs.

"You've already agreed to this. Dishing out compliments is no longer a prerequisite."

Air lodges in my throat, and I swallow thickly. His words are flowers and diamonds, and I'm just vulnerable enough to believe him.

I bring my hand to his unclothed back and run a light line up his spine, eyes darting between his. When my fingers reach the base of his hair, I stretch them around the back of his neck, and press down slightly. His mouth consumes mine again, a low growl traveling from his chest, past his throat, and into our kiss.

While he is distracted by the mating of our mouths, I drop my hand to the button of his jeans and squeeze my other arm from between my side and the seatback to help me unbutton his pants. I can't push them down, but I can at least loosen them enough to reach inside and cup him.

However, cupping is not quite possible as hard and full as he is. Instead, I wrap my fingers around the girth and move my fist along his length. I'm not sure who enjoys it more, nor who deepens the kiss because of the friction — we both seem to do it at the same time, our tongues delving in farther and harder.

Trenton's hips begin a slow grind, working himself in time with the movement of my grip. He breaks the kiss but only to drag his teeth along my bottom lip, lightly nipping.

After another soft peck, he hesitantly rises upright, and my hand slips out of his pants. He digs the condom out of his pocket and tears the wrapper open with his teeth.

Considering our slow and deliberate progress so far, I'm almost expecting this moment to be awkward and a mood killer, but when his gaze meets mine, it's anything but. A larger-than-life grin spreads across his handsome face, and he waggles his eyebrows as he rolls the condom on.

I laugh, but it comes out as a giggle. Like a damn teenage girl losing her virginity — all giddiness, nerves, and butterflies.

Trenton lowers over me, hands on either side of my head once more. Without any further preamble he centers himself between my thighs and enters me with one long, slow stroke, keeping with the pace of everything else. His eyes remain half-mast, locked on mine. On the second stroke, our lips meet. On the third, the two of us are overcome. My hands move to his ass to pull him in harder. His tongue spears into my mouth. We turn into desperate fiends. Trenton's hips work in tandem with the lifting of mine. Every delicious inch fills me, hitting each aching and throbbing spot hidden deep within. His body rubs against my clit perfectly with every thrust.

Hands slipping under his loosened jeans, skin on skin, I dig my nails into his flesh and draw them upward along the length of his back. My head angles upward, and a moan of release passes between my lips as we disconnect our mouths.

Knees bracketing his body, my legs tremble and insides clench around him, encouraging him to spill. His body listens to mine, reading every nuance, every cue. Obeying the demands of mine just as mine obeys the demands of his. His thrusting slows, and he engages in one final pump, burying deep, and releasing with a pulsating shudder.

Both my legs and arms become weak and useless. My knees fall open farther and my arms drop. One lands on his back, the other falls over the bench seat's edge, my knuckles landing on the floorboard.

Trenton slips out of me, one hand cupping himself to make sure the condom doesn't touch anything, and the other extended outward to help me sit. Once I do, though, he doesn't let go. Instead, he scoots backward, opens his door and steps out, dragging me along with him.

As soon as he's fully standing, the hand cupping his now-flaccid shaft drops to his side and he gives me a persuasive yank. Completely naked, body glistening with the sweat from both of us combined, I step out of his car. His hand drops mine, moves to my chin, and he pushes my head back, instantly boring his gaze into mine. "The deal was that we'd get together at my place." Those light-brown eyes dart quickly to the door leading inside then back to me. "We haven't quite made it there yet."

A stupid, ear to ear grin spreads across my flushed face. "Thank goodness it's not too far," I reply.

CHAPTER THIRTEEN

E arly morning light and the faint sound of birds chittering seep their way into my slumber. Instead of peeking my eyes open and stretching languidly, I shoot upward. The comforter and sheet that had been covering me falls to my hips, exposing my bare breasts.

Chest heaving, my hands grip the comforter and my gaze slowly travels sideways to check the state of my bed companion. Trenton is passed out, naked. The sunlight that peeks through his blinds highlights every ridge and dip… and that V. The one that didn't take me long to find once I—

Fuck.

Keeping as still as possible, my eyes scan the room until I find the digital clock.

Double fuck.

Heh… well, yeah…

It's too late — or early, rather. I stayed too long. If I don't get home soon, two very possessive men are going to hound my ass. Then, they'll find Trenton and hound his ass, too.

I gingerly slide my feet out of the covers and over the edge of the bed, then gently press myself off the mattress, darting a wary glance over my shoulder. If Trenton wakes up—

A soft groan leaves me as my attempt to stand pulls the sheet off him more. Exposing places. And things. And memories of last night. Or, rather, this morning. Just a few hours ago, in fact.

What the hell have I gotten myself into?

But... oh, God...

My eyes travel over him once more before I squeeze them shut tight and swallow hard.

Nope. Nope. Nope.

I slowly push the sheets off my lap and stand just as completely naked as Trenton. My throat tightens and heat burns across my cheeks and over my chest.

My clothes are still in his car.

Dammit.

I promptly go into problem-solving mode, studying his entire room in an attempt to figure out where he puts his clothes.

I might be brazen, but I'm not stupid. Double car garage? More than one bedroom? Someone else lives here, and the last thing I need is to walk out there with everything I have to offer on display.

I tiptoe to a dresser and open each drawer, one by one, until I find a shirt and pair of workout shorts.

The clothes are way too big on me, but I roll the waistband on the shorts until it's snug enough on my hips. The crew neck shirt hangs baggy over my shoulders, but at least the neckline is high enough my breasts won't pop out.

I pad back over to the bedside table and dig around for his keys, going ahead and taking a wild guess that he had likely locked his car doors.

Trenton shifts, flopping onto his belly, his bare ass displayed this time. A perfectly round—

Swiping my purse off the bedside table — at least I had enough sense not to leave that in his car, too — seeing his naked ass again is officially my cue to leave. With a grimace, I turn the doorknob, clenching my teeth and alternating glances from the gold ball to the bed and back again when the knob squeaks.

As soon as the door is open enough for me to slip through, I do exactly that. An immense amount of relief courses through me as I slowly close the door, holding the knob so the latch doesn't click until it is completely closed and I can release it without a sound.

When that is safely accomplished, I rest my forehead against the cool wood of the frame and take a few recovery breaths before turning around. Two steps forward and I slam hard into something. The collision sends me backward, my ass hitting Trenton's door.

Hand over my chest, fingers rubbing the spot of impact, I scarcely register that the thing I ran into was a person. Their elbow to be precise. This person is now grabbing my shoulders, dark-blue eyes darting everywhere, from the top of my messy hair to my bare feet.

"Holy shit, are you okay?" he squeaks. Without thinking, I reach out and clasp his mouth shut which, honestly, takes both of us by surprise. Our eyes widen into saucers. I yank my hand away and rub it down the side of my borrowed gym shorts.

He… looks… familiar. Those eyes? The color of dusk. His gaze moves to my face, eyes widening again once they land on—

Oh, shit.

My hand comes to the bruise on my cheek and I instinctively cover it. "I… I'm fine."

"Did my elbow hit your cheek?!" he lets out on a gasp.

"No! No. I got this last night."

His head tilts slightly and those familiar eyes look over my shoulder narrowing on Trenton's door.

Déjà vu slams into me. This is the guy I ran into outside of The Crowbar. Trenton's friend.

"Trenton gave you that?" he asks, eyebrows drawing inward as his gaze darts back and forth between mine.

"Oh! Gosh no. Um… bicycle accident."

"Bicyc—" His mouth starts to spread into a huge grin, but he presses his lips together to tame it down. "The girl from The Crowbar last night," he states, piecing the familiarity together just a beat after me.

Unlike our first run-in, this time he's only partially dressed and his hair is all mussed. The jutting hard-on that pokes into my upper thigh definitely… stands out… too. "A-are you going to let me go?" I ask, raising an eyebrow and flicking a glance at his hands that still grip my shoulders.

His gaze drops, and he jerks away. "Ah, sorry. You sure I didn't hurt you?" he asks, bringing his hand to the back of his neck and tilting a glance up at me from under the rim of his glasses as he gnaws on the bottom corner of his lip.

My fingers return to the now-delicate spot between my breasts. "Just a little tender is all; no big deal."

CHAPTER FOURTEEN

Hayes

Seeing as there's only about a foot separating us, it's evident I'm preventing her escape.

I can't decide whether I should find it funny that she's trying to pull a hit and run on my best friend or if I should be pissed off.

Either way, that's not why I've blocked her. If she wants to leave, she wants to leave. When I step back, though, chances she'll see my morning wood increase substantially.

The wood that was only slightly there when I walked out of the bedroom but instantly sprung to life, ready to get to work, when our warm bodies bumped against each other and my eyes found hers.

Her black hair is knotted and sticking up everywhere, her purse is slung across her torso, and she's wearing Trenton's clothes. Which I find amusing. And incredibly sexy.

Making matters worse, the thin white of his shirt doesn't do much to cover her dark, hardened nipples.

"Hungry?" I ask, trying to keep my focus on her nose, because if I continue to look anywhere else, I might just rupture on the spot.

Since my eyes are still somewhat blurry, and my mind is still a bit hazy from sleep despite the shocking turn of events, my cock might very well get confused and act like it's in a wet dream or something.

Then we'd have a really big mess on our hands. Or… in my briefs more likely.

"No, thank you." She holds up a set of keys and jingles them.

Trenton's house keys.

Not only was she sneaking out of his bedroom, but she was also considering hijacking his car? Looking over my shoulder, she clears her throat. "I… uhm… my clothes are in Trenton's car." My eyes drop to her mouth as she bares her teeth in a cute grimace. "Plus, I can't usually eat this early."

"Hot chocolate? Tea? Coffee? I'll make it while we wait for him to wake up… which might take a while."

Unless you start sucking his cock. Rumor has it that seems to work.

Not liking the idea of waiting, her throat moves over a nervous swallow and her fingers constantly fiddle with the keys as she grows more anxious by the second.

"Those are his house keys," I explain. "He hides his car keys. I kinda stole the MC once when we were in high school and hid it in an alleyway. He hasn't trusted me since."

This changes her mood instantly, and she barks out a laugh, quickly covering her mouth to muffle the sound.

Morning wood sufficiently softened for a time, I finally step aside so she can get by.

"Sure, thanks. Coffee sounds great." The words come out quiet and unsure, her shoulders a little more curved in now than they were before.

She walks past me nonetheless, and I follow behind. No longer able to look at her nose, I attempt to keep my focus on the kitchen ahead, instead.

Remembering I am still only in my boxers, I skid short, clear my throat, and say, "Don't run away. I just need to get some pants on. Kitchen is on the right."

Her head bobs, and I dash into my bedroom and hop into a pair of sweats as quickly as possible.

When I get to the kitchen, she's sitting on top of the counter, heels propped on the edge of a couple drawers.

Since I'm the only one in the house that drinks coffee, Trenton insisted I get a set up that doesn't take up a ton of room. A bit of research helped me decide on a pour-over system. There are several pieces, but everything is small and easy to store.

After grabbing a couple of mugs and measuring water into a gooseneck kettle, I turn on the stove burner and heat the water while collecting everything else I need: scale, dripper, pitcher, and grinder.

The process is relaxing and my favorite way to start the day, so I easily fall into the routine. "How do you take your coffee?" I ask, scooping beans into the hand grinder and setting it on the scale. She doesn't answer, so I dart a quick glance over my shoulder.

Her head tilts sideways, and the spot between her eyebrows wrinkles. "Are you doing a science experiment?" she asks.

The question catches me off guard. "A sci—ohhh, no. Well… I mean, there's science behind it, I guess. Pour-over coffee?"

She raises an eyebrow and shakes her head.

"Prepare to be amazed." I put on my biggest smile and wave my hands like a magician, the measuring scoop my wand.

Shit… Crow was right — I'm awkward as hell.

She chuckles, and I continue my tasks. "Cream? Sugar?" I ask, peeking at her again.

"Oh, um… I'm not hard to please. Surprise me?" Her hands come to the edge of the counter, and she curls her fingers around the lip, leaning forward to peer over my shoulder as I start manually cranking the handle.

I turn around and lean back against the counter opposite so she can watch what I am doing. When everything is in sight, she straightens, hands returning to her lap.

By the time I'm done grinding the beans and pouring the grounds inside the filtered dripper, the kettle is whistling, ready to go. I turn off the burner, lift the kettle, and swirl in the first pour. "Gotta let the grounds bloom," I state matter-of-factly.

Thirty or so awkward seconds crawl between us while my ass rests against the edge of the counter, super-manly gooseneck kettle in hand, patiently waiting for just long enough to pass.

Whistling the tune to a popular old game show, I stare at the ceiling waiting. When my mental timer goes off, I steal another quick glance at her before adjusting to my hip.

The cute side-grin she's sporting does some crazy shit to my heart, and it takes extra effort to look away this time.

I swirl in the second pour of water to agitate the grounds, give it a few seconds, then continue pouring water in at a steady pace until the kettle is almost empty.

While waiting for the liquid to filter into the pitcher, I use the small amount remaining to warm our mugs by swirling it along the inside of each, making sure they're coated in heat so the coffee won't cool right away when served. After letting that sit for a few seconds and dumping it out, I open the butter dish, slice off a teaspoon or so of butter, place it in her mug, then do the same with a tablespoon for mine.

When the coffee finishes, I remove the dripper, toss the filter and grounds into the trash can, and pour us both a cup, leaving just enough room in the mug to add a bit of coconut milk.

Once the coconut milk is added, I move to the silverware drawer to get my electric whisk but am met with her bent knees. In the flow of routine, I'd momentarily forgotten she was sitting there. Before I realize it, her knees are at about my shoulder level. With them slightly open, it's practically impossible for my eyes not to drift between her legs.

Okay, Hayes.

Do not make this weird.

My focus drifts down farther to the drawer. I lift my hand, dragging my finger over her ankle in a silent suggestion that she lift her foot.

She does, and I almost let out an audible exhale of relief. Not quite catching myself in time, an odd choke-cough comes out instead.

Dammit.

Before I can embarrass myself more, I snatch the whisk and back away. She immediately props her heel on the drawer again.

Coffee, coffee, coffee.

Coffee.

Right.

I return to the opposite counter, press the button on the miniature electric whisk and blend each of our

94

coffees until the tops are perfectly frothy. Then, I quickly move to the sink and rinse off the whisk under running water.

Instead of putting it away in the drawer, though, I decide to set it on the countertop beside the sink.

Mission accomplished, I grab both cups of coffee and hand hers over.

She gives me a soft smile and brings the mug to her mouth, dipping her upper lip into the creamy froth. I turn around and palm my cock, tossing a casual look — and mumbling a curse — at the ceiling.

CHAPTER FIFTEEN

Remi

Butter in coffee is a new experience for me. It's surprisingly good. Rich and creamy. For a time, I'm content to sit here and sip, not wanting it to get too cool by waiting.

Trenton's friend, whose name I still don't know, stands about as far away from me as possible, leaning against the opposite counter and angled just enough that he is blocking the clock on the stove from my view. I can swing a little bit of time, since Jude and Porter aren't early birds. But not much.

If push comes to shove, I suppose waltzing in the house like the adult I am and telling them I decided to go for an early-morning stroll on the beach is always an option. Trouble is, I locked my bedroom door and will have to climb back through the window to get in there. Unless, of course, I jimmy the lock, but that would undoubtedly raise their suspicions.

There's also the issue of my attire. Not sure how well my story will be received upon showing up wearing another man's clothing.

The coffee guy clears his throat and snaps me out of my thoughts. "Do you like it?" he asks, holding up his mug and quirking an eyebrow.

"Oh… yeah… I do. Thank you." I bite at the inside of my cheek before taking another sip. He seems to follow me motion for motion, which is weird and cute all at the same time. The steam from his drink builds under his glasses but clears when he brings the mug back down toward his stomach.

"Remi? Is that your name?" he asks next, and I swallow hard over the most recent gulp.

"Yeah. Trenton told you all about me, huh?"

"Mm-hmm," he hums.

My eyes dart everywhere but at the friend of the guy I just slept with.

Well… this is incredibly awkward.

After a moment longer, I finally decide to say something. "Yeah… he told me all about you, too."

His eyebrows rise above the frame of his eyeglasses, and I swear the tick of a smile lifts the corner of his lips as he takes another sip. "Did he?"

"Oh yes. Revealed all your dirty secrets."

He almost chokes on a swallow. "On the first night?" he gasps, drawing a laugh from me.

Truth is, Trenton didn't do much talking at all other than our texting last night. "Said you drank your feelings away on account of so rudely bumping into me. But, he failed to mention your name."

He chuckles. "Now that's not surprising." His chest lifts and falls as he takes a deep breath before pushing off the counter and stepping toward me, hand extended.

I accept it and he gives my hand a single shake. "Hayes. And I actually don't drink much at all. Only occasionally." His thumb grazes mine as he pulls his hand away and brings it to join the other in cupping his mug.

"Nice to meet you, Hayes." I give him a genuine smile. "Sorry about last night."

"About last night?"

"The noise—" My focus drops to the hem of Trenton's shirt for a split-second as I begin to fidget with the material. "Nope, never mind." If he isn't privy to what happened between us last night, I'd rather not make him uncomfortable by drawing attention to it.

Hayes musses his hair and presses his lips together to hide a smile as he returns to the counter. I dart a quick glance over his shoulder before he blocks the clock again. Tapping his ear, he responds, "Headphones. I fell asleep at my computer, gaming."

Guess he is privy after all.

"Oh, okay. Whew." To exaggerate the whew, I wipe my forehead with the back of my hand. Hayes laughs. "So, do you make breakfast for every woman Trenton brings home?"

Hayes blows a raspberry from between his lips, shrugs, and clears his throat. "Uh… hm… y-yeah…

well sometimes. Depends… you know? I mean… no… I guess you wouldn't… know."

I raise a single eyebrow and take another drink of the coffee — a bigger one this go-round because it's cooling and I'm running out of time. Hayes seems to be beating himself up for his inability to say, *"Why yes, Trenton fucks all sorts of women, and I'm here in the mornings to pick up their shattered hearts when he tosses them out."* I decide to help a little by changing the subject: "So, you drive a Bimmer?"

His mouth gapes and he blinks at me a couple times. He picks his jaw up off the floor and says, "Most girls either don't know what kind of car it is, or they call it a Beamer. What planet do you hail from?"

Playing the uninformed, ditzy female clearly isn't in my wheelhouse. That's not the first time my automotive knowledge has slipped. But once you know, you know. "Greetings, Earthling," I chuckle.

Hayes rolls his eyes. Then, something dawns on me. The profile name on that car forum — Hazerbeam. The tip of my tongue itches to say something. To ask if that's him. A play on a sciencey term like laser beam? But twisted in a way to relate to both his name and his car? Clever. I like this guy.

"Yeah… I once knew someone who was a bike enthusiast. They taught me the bikes are called Beamers, and the cars are called Bimmers." A memory of Dad correcting me the first time floats to the surface, and I brush it away. Hayes is right, most people — men and women alike — just lump everything into the Beamer category.

Of course, I want to ask something along the topic of races or meets, but I choose not to. If these guys are part of the club Jude and Porter are looking for, it's not your typical underground street racing club. There's money involved, and a lot of it. Clubs like those treasure their anonymity. Ask too soon, and it might raise a red flag.

Hayes steps forward, approaches the sink beside me, and cleans out his mug. I hop down from the counter and take the opposite basin, waiting until he's done before flicking the faucet over to my side to wash my own.

Hayes's still-sudsy hand slips through the stream of water and his fingers wrap over mine to steal it back.

A crash from behind alarms us both and we jump apart, spinning around. Trenton hops through the hallway on one foot as he attempts to put on pants. "Dude," he says, "I think I just became the victim of a hit and run."

"The one you swore was going to be your wife one day?" Hayes hollers in return as Trenton struggles, bouncing off the walls, focus riveted on the floor so as not to lose balance.

"Yeah…" the word trails as he finally looks up and sees that I'm still here. His gaze drifts down my body, taking in my borrowed clothes, and his lips hitch up at the side.

Hayes returns to his task at the sink and finishes cleaning the mug he'd managed to sneak from my hands amid the distraction.

"Carlo got your clothes?" Trenton winks, playing on the *cat got your tongue* idiom.

I narrow a glare at him. "Was that planned?"

Trenton shrugs. "Can't get on bended knee and propose marriage if you're not here to accept the ring. Had to secure the deal."

He steps forward and drops to a knee, running his hands under my — his — shorts and up my outer thighs before dragging his teeth over the mesh material at the waistband area and tugging a little. His warm breath against my skin makes my stomach jerk in response. My eyes dart to Hayes. Instead of his attention being riveted on the dishes as it was just a moment ago, he now leans against the counter beside us, watching in amusement.

Trenton's hands leave the shorts. His fingers come to a stray string that had been snagged free on the mesh, and he plucks it free. The elastic waistband pulls forward and falls back against me with a snap. He then takes my left hand in his, wraps the string around my ring finger, and tucks the end under and through to create a small knot.

Still on bended knee, he grins up at Hayes. "Look, bro, I finally tied the knot!"

Hayes simply raises a brow and crosses his arms. Trenton returns his attention to me, eyes sparkling in delight. "I looked everywhere and didn't see the leash you promised to bring, so this'll have to do."

The leash…

Oh!

A laugh bubbles from me, and I rub the top of his head. My left hand still held by his, he pushes up to his feet, brings my knuckles to his mouth, and gives them a light kiss. "Good morning," he says with a grin as his sepia-colored eyes meet mine from a still slightly down-turned head.

"Good morning." I chuckle.

The girly kind.

"I see you two have gotten acquainted already." Trenton lets go of my hand and gestures to the now-clean mugs.

The motion draws my eyes back to the clock on the stove, and every bit of that coffee nearly comes back up. "We did… and…" I'm already hating that I have to legit get out of here. The timing is terrible. But, in my defense, we weren't supposed to have *that* much fun last night. I'm not supposed to be here still.

Both guys wait for me to finish what I had started to say. "I need to go," I reveal with a grimace. "I… didn't tell my brother I was heading out last night, and

I would really like to get back before he realizes I'm gone and begins to worry."

They both give me curious looks. I get it. I do. What grown woman is still held accountable to her sibling? "Look… it's complicated."

Trenton nods slowly a couple times, his gaze drifting over my face. Hayes rubs the back of his neck. The two share a glance, and Hayes gives Trenton some sort of slight head tilt and shoulder lift. Then, Trenton holds his hand out.

Despite not understanding what just passed between them, I take it anyway. "Okay, Cinderella. Let's get your glass slippers back on, hmm?" With a grin, Trenton leans toward me, places the hand he had grabbed onto his chest, and lowers his voice, "And your bra, and that sexy thong, and those tight pants… and that racing shirt."

I press my lips together to stifle the smile that lifts higher with each mentioned article of clothing. "Okay, okay… point made."

Hayes unabashedly stands nearby watching and listening to everything. Trenton's lips brush along my jawline as he straightens. And when my eyes dip, snagging a glimpse of Hayes, I swear I see the briefest lick of his lips before his upper teeth catch for a heartbeat on his bottom lip.

Hmm. Interesting.

Trenton slings my hand over his shoulder and tucks me into his side, my purse wedged between us. He darts a backward glance at Hayes.

"Come help me jimmy my car will you?" he says with a groan.

Hayes chokes and stutters. "Y-you… why?"

"Act cool, man," he whisper-yells to his friend as we approach the garage door. "Maybe she won't realize I locked my keys in there along with her clothes."

"You what?!" both Hayes and I ask at the same time.

Trenton comes to a dead stop. "You distracted the hell out of me!"

Damn it's hard to be mad at him and freak out, because he makes it so easy to not care about the consequence. Plus, he's right, I am partially to blame. I didn't exactly tell him last night that I needed to get out of here by a certain time. But that's also because I didn't anticipate staying long enough for it to matter.

As if Hayes can sense my building panic at how long this might take, he states, "How about I take her home?"

My shoulders instantly loosen. Trenton darts a look at me and turns us to face Hayes. "Hey, that's okay with me, if you're good with it?" he directs toward me.

With a glance down at the baggy white shirt and loose shorts, I have a tough decision to make. Leave now, without my clothes, and sneak back into my room before Jude and Porter wake up? Or, show up late, wearing something that proves I was out for more than just a stroll on the beach, and have a lot of uncomfortable explaining to do?

After a moment's consideration, I decide sneaking back in is the least risky approach — assuming I don't get caught, of course. "Yeah... I would actually really appreciate that."

CHAPTER SIXTEEN

"Trenton mentioned you're new to the area. Moved here from California with your brother and a friend?" Hayes makes small talk while we navigate back to the beach side of the city. His fingers tap a silent rhythm on the steering wheel. "If you don't have any other plans today, I can drive you around a bit. Give you the grand tour?"

The offer surprises me, considering our awkward start this morning. "That sounds great actually. If you don't have anywhere to be, and you don't mind waiting for me to take a shower first? I could really use one." My nose crinkles.

"Yeah, you could. You smell like Trenton." Hayes wrinkles his own nose to mimic mine, successfully receiving the laugh he'd been aiming for.

"That… does not surprise me," I whisper, unsure how this thing between Hayes and Trenton works. He'd said they were friends in high school. Guess when you're friends with someone like Trenton for that long, you probably get used to his antics after a time.

"So, does he often propose to his one-night stands?" I ask with a chuckle. My hands run down the seat's custom harness straps. Racing evidence is slowly stacking up the more time I spend around these guys. Unlike Trenton's, this car isn't a sleeper — you can tell from the outside that Hayes tinkers — but on the inside? Racing seats with harness-style belts. The four-point system that goes over each shoulder and buckles at the pelvis.

Part of me questions if the car is even road legal with seats like these. But, surely there's no reason for racing seats if he's not... well... racing. Right? Without looking under the hood or asking him directly, though, I have no way of knowing.

"Uh. Nope." His delayed response has me confused for a moment, tricking my mind into thinking he'd responded to my mental question instead of what I'd asked about Trenton. "Guess you... impressed him."

"Hmm... I wonder which part. Maybe it was when I did that one thing with my tongue." A half-grin tugs at my lips. I was trying to be funny, but when Hayes doesn't respond, I peek cautiously in his direction. Instead of his fingers tapping the steering wheel, they're now wrapped tightly around it.

"Sorry." Cheeks burning, I return my focus to the road, eyes spotting a real estate ad of a man and his wife standing beside a vintage truck. Tacky tagline and all.

Maybe Jude and I can become a team.
Sell houses.
For the love of God, not vehicles.

Suffering yet another unfortunate reminder of why I'm involved with this new group of guys, my gut knots.

"You're good. Tell me more," he says, shooting me a sideways glance and smile.

Thankful for the continued banter, I'm quick to reply. "Well, when I twist—"

"Kidding. I was kidding." He laughs. A real laugh, not an offended one, instantly lightening the mood.

"Crossed a line, hm?" I flash him a grin and a quick brow bounce.

Realizing my choice of words has the potential to turn our conversation toward cars, I cast my first race-related question: "Speaking of crossing a line... do you? Ever 'line up,' I mean?" To build on my reasoning for the question, I drag my fingers over the harness straps.

When he doesn't offer a response and a dense quiet fills the cab, I know I've touched on a hush topic.

This type of silence — the uncomfortable, gawky type — always sets me on edge. I much prefer bumbling backchat. The fact it was caused by the very topic I've been struggling to tap into tautens the knot in my stomach and a fine layer of sweat dampens my palms.

"So, I guess you'll be the best man then, hm?" I ask, attempting to revert back to Trenton — the only thing other than cars that we have in common.

"Heh. Yeah. I better be," he replies. One of his hands leaves the wheel and lands on the back of his neck. "What's your address?"

Okay… so maybe Trenton is a subject best left alone, too.

The dismissal throws me a bit, but his question throws me more. One, because I don't actually want him to drop me off at home. Two, because… I don't have my address memorized yet. "Drop me off on the corner of Beach and Sunset. I need to pick up something from the small general store there anyway. Then I can just meet you back there in, like, thirty minutes?"

"Okay, yeah. I'll swing into the gas station a few blocks down from there and fill up," he responds.

After ten achingly uncomfortable minutes of wordless driving, we're at our destination. I work myself out of the harness, grab my purse, and step out with a hasty, "Thanks! See you in a bit."

I pop into the general store and watch through the tinted glass as he drives away. As soon as the purple, black, and white abstract pattern of his bumper is out of view, I leave and walk around to the rear of the building.

The store backs up to the street we just moved to and is directly across from the Regency Hotel where Trenton picked me up last night. Our new place is only about eight houses down on the right, so I jog the short way, hurry around to the back yard, climb the fence, leap to the shed roof, and push myself up and into the awaiting open window of my bedroom.

With a deep inhale and exhale, I slide down the wall beside the window until I am on my butt, knees up.

A single, rogue tear trickles free.

The excitement and distraction of doing something fun — something for me — had proved a good diversion. Aside from scattered reminders in things like billboard ads and aftermarket car parts, I hadn't realized my heart was struggling with the unfairness of the forceful demands I've been subjected to.

Not until I hit the floor in my bedroom and see that my door is still locked and the room is empty. The fear that I would be caught was real. Here I am, a woman in her early twenties, terrified because she decided to leave the house. But that fear was something I stubbornly refused to feed. Something I still refuse to feed. Refusal or not, my subconscious bends under the injustice. Aches because of it. That single tear is its only way of screaming in defiance.

Maybe you should just talk to Jude.

Tell him the truth.

Do you really think that by throwing these guys under the bus things will instantly get better? That Porter will just stop? That the truth will just go away?

No. Even if my secrets remain buried, the truth will always lurk. Ever present. By following through, though, I'll at least help secure a small bit of Jude's future and our father's legacy and make Jude proud of me in the process. Perhaps when the shit hits the fan, my willingness to be involved will serve as a bit of reparation for the horrible things I have — and continue — to do unbeknownst to him.

I wipe my damp cheek, push off the floor, toss my purse onto the bed, and enter the bathroom. Stripping off Trenton's clothes, that pesky fear brushes against my nerves. A sluice of 'what ifs' consume my thoughts:

What if I'd been caught?

What if Porter saw me in another man's clothes?

What if these guys don't have the information I need?

What if they do?

What if?

What if?

What if?

CHAPTER SEVENTEEN

Wken I step over the threshold to exit my bedroom, Porter is standing at the glass sliders on the side of the level that overlooks the balcony, intently watching something outside.

Shit that was a close call. He's up early — and fully alert nonetheless.

My stomach twists as I dart a glance over my shoulder at the clock on my bedside table to make sure I hadn't gone over the thirty minutes I'd promised Hayes. If I don't show up in time, will he start driving around looking for me and somehow figure out which house is mine? Or will he give up and leave altogether?

Getting into my bedroom, taking a quick shower, blow-drying my hair, and getting dressed didn't take long at all, thank goodness. I still have about five minutes to spare.

I walk through the hallway and scan the kitchen. Jude isn't in there, nor is he in the fireplace room, so I simply continue toward the door. Toward Porter.

Approaching, I ask, "What's going on?" But the glint of the morning sun bouncing off a semi cab catches my eye and answers the question before Porter can. He looks down at me with a brief glance before returning his attention to the newly-arrived car hauler.

Unsurprisingly, Jude is up in arms with the driver.

When I turn to walk back into the kitchen, Porter's fingers wrap around my upper arm and he pulls me to him.

My entire body tenses, but I look straight up into his eyes, feigning strength. He watches me for a second, gaze drifting slowly over my face. His fingers release my arm and come up to my cheek to brush over the sensitive bruise. "Maybe next time you'll only open up that pretty mouth of yours when I tell you to, hmm?"

My nose and throat burn with building rage. And here I was convincing myself it was just because he was drunk. That he didn't usually do stuff like this.

Then again, we had never lived together before either. Our "forays" were exclusive to him coming over to visit Dad or Jude. Or, in the rare occurrence I would ride with Jude to Porter's apartment for the night if some sort of party or car event was taking place. And since those times were few and far between, our interactions were simple. He'd woo me into bed, and I'd crawl in obedience.

Why? Because I thought I loved him. He'd only ever hit me once, and he was wasted then. Completely smashed. The next day he couldn't even remember it had happened.

This... this is not the Porter I thought we were moving in with. Money hungry? Yes. Horny bastard? Absolutely. But an abuser? Guess I've still been too trusting — too naive — to peg him as such.

Truth is, with his bold statement, I'm already absolutely terrified to lash out with what I'd really like to say. I'm too emotionally tired today; his treatment of me last night still lingers in my psyche to where I'm not sure I can deal with the repercussions of another physical — or mental — assault.

Instead, I don't say anything at all, replying with a demure drop of my gaze.

The upper level where the stilted deck meets the entrance begins to vibrate. Porter drops his hand, and my eyes dart toward the glass doors. Jude storms up the steps, two at a time. When he slides the door open, I duck my head, letting my hair fall over my face, and quickly double back toward my room to put a little makeup on before he sees the bruise and I'm forced to lie yet again.

I make quick work of the job. The proof isn't horrible looking or anything, but the red and slight purple is just enough to stand out against my bronzed skin tone.

Mission accomplished, I leave my room once again. This time, Porter and Jude are both in the kitchen leaning against the island.

"Everything good?" I ask, directing the question at Jude.

Jude rolls his eyes. "Guy put a few miles on the Skyline. Swears it didn't happen. Tried to chalk it up to rolling it onto the rack." Jude scoffs. "Last I checked, trailer racks aren't four miles long. Fucking independent truckers."

I raise an eyebrow at him as I open the refrigerator. "Can you blame him?" I egg. The version of Skyline he owns is one of only five street legal ones in the entire United States. Of course someone jumped at the chance to take it for a spin.

My eyes scan the refrigerator's contents, searching for something easy to snack on before meeting with Hayes.

"Well no," he says, slumping his shoulders.

"So, are you mad at the driver or at yourself for cutting corners and going independent?" Yeah, I know how to get under his skin. In the best kind of way.

Jude glowers at me. "Smart ass."

I grab an orange, bump the fridge closed with my hip, then flash him a super-sized grin as I walk backward toward the door

"See you guys for dinner; I'm going to the beach."
I salute them and steal the opportunity to slip out before either can find an excuse to keep me here.

As soon as I'm in the driveway, I sneak under the deck and run my palm along the leather seat of my bike. Praise the Trucking Gods, she arrived safely.

Knowing I am definitely late now, I keep the reunion short and sweet, give her a friendly pat, and jog away toward the end of the block, peeling and eating my snack en route. When I round the corner, Hayes is waiting there as planned. An unexpected, excited smile spreads across my face as our eyes connect through his windshield.

He waits until I hop inside and get situated before flashing me a return smile. The short separation seems to have been just enough to erase the bit of tension from earlier.

Even still, neither of us say anything as he navigates out of the parking lot and onto the road. His hand moves to the shifter, and I hustle to buckle the harness before he throws her into the next gear, squealing the tires and swerving as he thrusts us forward.

The grin and shake of my head betray my feigned apathy.

Fucking car guys.

CHAPTER EIGHTEEN

"**H**ow long have you been here?" he asks.

"Less than a week," I answer, immediately noting how horrible that appears considering I just slept with his best friend.

When he throws a raised eyebrow at me, I grimace. "I realize how that must come off. I've definitely had one-night stands a time or two, but it's not like a recreational activity I participate in on a regular basis or anything."

Hayes taps his fingers on the steering wheel. Once again, the silence makes me more anxious than embarrassing conversations. Naturally, I dig myself in deeper. "Trenton… he… I had a really good time. He ticked off a lot of my boxes, you know?"

I hadn't meant to end the babbling as a question, but it was out, hovering between us before it could be amended. Sure, I wish I could say something like, *"Plus he made me feel safe and desired and took my pain and heartache away,"* but I decide not to. I've already painted myself in poor light; no need to make it worse.

After my rambling, I anticipate yet another increasingly awkward car ride as he turns around and takes me back to the store. Instead, he places his hand over mine and moves it to the gearshift.

"Do you know how to drive a stick?" he asks.

Surprised at the sudden change of topic, the somewhat heated way it was delivered along with a hint of innuendo, and the unexpected feel of his hand over mine, my head whips in his direction, eyes like saucers.

When the realization of how what he said was delivered sinks in, he stutters, "Heh, nope... did not mean it that way."

I burst into laughter, incredibly thankful for yet another reprieve from the strange and unruly friction that continues to swell between us.

His fingers slip between mine as he grips the knob under my hand.

"Yes, I know how to drive a *manual*."

He flicks a quick look at me, the faintest of smiles ticking on his lips.

"Good," he says. "Then you know that sometimes you have to react — to switch gears — based on how the car and the situation feels. Not on what all the other, external elements are doing." Hayes clears his throat and drops his voice: "Or *saying*, for what it's worth."

Ah, so this is somehow his way of making me feel better about this strange triangle in which I've found myself involved.

He tilts his head toward the glove compartment. "Grab the noise cancellers and put them on."

I pop the box with my free hand, remove the earmuffs, and snap it closed with my wrist before attempting to slide them on one-handed. Hayes watches me struggle, amused and apparently having no intention of letting my other hand go to aid in my effort.

I give him a playful glare but still manage to accomplish the task.

He moves his left foot closer to his seat and steers with his knee while leaning over to pluck open one side of my muffs. "You switch gears; I've got everything else handled. No peeking at the speedometer."

Mouth partly open, I gape at him. Yeah, I know how to drive a stick. I know how to drive just about anything, in fact. Put me in that damn car hauler and I'd probably get the job done. But do it without watching the gauges or hearing the inflection of it revving as the car basically screams at you to shift gears? And risk someone else's car while trying?

No.

Nope.

When he sees my features morph with panic, his eyes light up, and little wrinkles bunch at the corners. If I could hear him, I'd guess he's laughing. Using his knee to steer again, sound assaults me when he lifts the muff. "Don't screw up my car, Remi," he says before letting go and shrouding me in silence again.

The car jerks forward, and I'm too stunned to react. Hayes anticipates this, though; his hand squeezes mine as he shifts.

My gaze bolts toward him, and he cocks an eyebrow. Chest heaving, I give him a sharp nod. He doesn't rush this time; the slight increase in speed vibrates beneath my thighs, and I watch the billboards get closer as he accelerates at a steady pace.

Pressure on my hand and the jostle of the shaft wiggles its way into my overactive thoughts, indicating I've dropped the ball yet again. Frustration fills me, but I know instantly why I missed it. I'm too focused on everything else: How fast the lane markings are passing; How long it took us to get from one billboard to the next; How quickly we're approaching the car in front of us.

Having had enough proof that Hayes will pick up where I fall short, I slam my eyes shut and let my head fall back against the seat. Instead of depending on my sense of sight, I focus on the nuances of the car accelerating and his warm hand on mine — nothing more.

The vibration increases slightly, and I realize that's my cue. However, when his hand doesn't close over mine, I doubt my assessment.

On second thought, if I shift at the wrong time, he'll feel the motion of my hand and stop me. I take a quick chance and maneuver the shaft into the next gear. The car gives a slight jerk and the vibration smooths out before slowly humming to life again as he increases speed. Calmer now, more relaxed, my body molds into the seat. Hayes seems to sense this change in me, and his hand loosens a bit. He still keeps it there just in case, but his fingers no longer grip the knob from between mine.

I tend to give guys a hard time about their obsessions where vehicles are concerned, but really I'm not much better. There's just something about the rev of an engine and the rove of tires over asphalt.

And Hayes has me intentionally concentrating on those exact elements. Now hyper-aware of every little sensation, the buzz of acceleration travels through my thighs and straight into my core. The light brush of his thumb against mine doesn't escape my notice and only heightens my internal, physical responses.

This time, when the car rumbles with that anticipated, exaggerated whir, I'm ready. Far more confident now, I adjust the gearshift as necessary. The car does a telltale jolt as it completes the shifting process.

Hayes's hand remains relaxed and trusting draped over mine.

Having kept tally, and knowing that we aren't exactly on a high speed road, I surmise we will no longer be shifting into a higher gear.

Less than a minute later, the car pitches forward, nose dipping at the front to indicate we're decelerating. My eyes snap open and my knee-jerk reaction is to drop into a lower gear. We're approaching a light and Hayes is steadily slowing down. Out of habit, my gaze flicks to the speedometer, only to see an envelope now blocks the numbers. I take that as a hint to close my eyes again. When I do, the car feels as though it is coming to a stop much quicker than it appeared visually. I downshift again and again until I can no longer feel the road humming beneath us, just the rhythmic pulsations of his car and the heat from his hand.

I peek one eye open at him, and he reaches over with his other hand to pull the noise cancellers off. After he tosses them in the back seat, he removes his hand, and I return mine to my lap, wiping the slight dampness from my palm onto my jeans.

CHAPTER NINETEEN

Hayes and I have a great time. With so much area to cover and so many interesting hidden places only locals would know about, I don't even realize how late it has gotten until the sun dips beneath the buildings.

He had taken me out to lunch at this great waterfront restaurant that had a band playing, then showed me his favorite place to get dessert — an ice cream parlor serving freeze-dried dots of ice cream similar to what astronauts might eat. I got a good kick out of that since it was so very "nerdy" and so very Hayes — all awkwardness and a whole lot of smart.

Ironically enough, it isn't until I recognize it's past time for me to go home that my mind strays to cars and racing again. Aside from the evaded question about lining up, and the analogy lesson he taught me about trusting my instincts in the beginning of the day, I hadn't asked anything more about the topic, and he hadn't brought anything up.

Right now, we're cruising slow on their much-less-grandiose version of Sunset Boulevard. Definitely not as epic, but still beautiful, though. My arm rests on the track of the open window, hand dangling outside just enough to where I can wiggle my fingers in the breeze.

I track the line where the sky meets the gulf between passing buildings. Hayes has music playing with the volume up just enough to create a mood but low enough to where I can't make out the song.

Memories of Cali drift into my thoughts — of riding down Sunset Boulevard more times than I can count. With my dad. With Jude. With Porter.

The irony surrounding this situation with Trenton and Hayes does not slip my mind. The fact that my only leads — well, them and that Crow guy — have both somehow already become what I might consider friends — the inevitable "firsts" who take you in and befriend you when you're new to an area.

A knot forms in my stomach, twisting and dripping with regret. Becoming friends with my leads is not how this sleuthing thing was supposed to unfold.

But even so, deep in the crevices of those wandering thoughts, a small bit of hope sprouts — hope that they aren't involved in this underground racing club.

"Curfew?" Hayes pulls me back to the present before my heart and mind get too carried away with overthinking.

"Heh, wouldn't that be something? A twenty-three-year-old woman, bound by a curfew."

Hayes shrugs and darts a tentative side-eye in my direction. He's smart enough to know something is up with the puffy cheekbone and being dropped off at a corner store. Guess this is his way of checking in?

"Mm, kinda but not really. Promised my brother I would handle dinner tonight. As long as I get back before he gets hangry, we should be good."

Hayes chuckles and nods, tapping at the side of the steering wheel, a nervous tick of his when he has something to say but doesn't know how to deliver the thought. Which… is quite often.

Once he does get on the topic of something he enjoys, though, it is no holds barred; his eyes light up, framed by glasses, and his gestures become animated. When silence falls, though, the awkwardness is nearly all-consuming. It's… cute… and sweet in its own way.

"The sun sets in about thirty minutes; think you have enough time to watch it with me?" he asks.

Cruising, lunch, ice cream, more cruising, and now he wants to watch the sunset? Can this day possibly get anymore perfect?

"Yeah… That would be amazing actually. Maybe I can just call a few pizzas in when we get there, then pick them up on the way back? That way, when I show up late, I can walk in bearing the gift of food, and there will be less room for complaints."

"Sounds like a solid plan," he responds. "There's a great pizza place down the road from where I picked you up earlier and a public beach access point right across the street from there."

"Perfect." I know exactly what pizza place he's referring to, because it's the one Jude had jokingly mentioned taking a job at when we were discussing our lack of options for making a name for the Delancey's in this area. We hadn't tried their pizzas, though, so ordering from there now falls into line nicely with this intricate story I'm weaving.

Jude and Porter assume I've been on foot all day. If I were to have walked all the way to the pizza place, picked up the pizzas, then hitched a ride back with a random person, the plot should work just right.

A stack of pizzas to match the stack of lies.

Again that understanding twists tightly within me.

Seeing as Hayes had already turned the car around quite some time ago, we aren't too terribly far away from the spot he's talking about. Within five minutes or so, he pulls into the parking lot of what appears to be a closed dance club. Off season, is my guess.

We get out, he locks up, and we walk around the side of the building to the beach behind. As if it's the most natural thing in the world, we then sit side by side with our knees up in a spot not quite where the water has dampened and compacted the sand, but not quite where it's too soft and messy either.

The sun is still a smidgen too high to set, so I take the opportunity to slip my phone out of my pocket, search for the number to the pizza place, and make the call.

When it starts ringing, Hayes snatches the phone from my hand. No playful smile, no warning, just a quick swipe before situating the phone between his shoulder and ear. Arms draped between his knees, he absently toys with his keys.

A woman's voice filters through the line and Hayes straightens, "Is Lainie delivering tonight?" he asks. The voice on the other line responds. "Yeah. We're near the water behind the club." He then cranks his head to the side and addresses me with a low voice, "What are you ordering?"

"Uhm." I blow a raspberry from my lips. "Let's do one with all meat and two with everything?"

Hayes repeats the order, provides a name and credit card number from memory, the voice responds, then Hayes hangs up and hands me the phone with an accomplished grin.

Looking down, I let my hair fall over the amused smile on my face. How is it that these guys make it so easy to…

Forget?

Let go?

Relax?

I lift my gaze to the sun that still threatens to set but has a bit of life left before committing.

To remind me of how things used to be.

126

That's what it is. They so easily bring out the part of me that was stripped away. That alternate Remi is just below the surface, anyway. Not too far. So, I guess it makes sense. Or maybe I just ache for a semblance of life how it was before everything fell apart?

And they provide a tease of that salvation.

CHAPTER TWENTY

Hayes scoots over closer and nudges his shoulder into mine.

A ridiculous, school-girl smile creeps up across my face. "Thanks for everything today. Breakfast, lunch, dinner, the cruise, ice cream…" — my voice trails and lowers — "the lesson."

Hayes shrugs and gives me one of his cute side-smiles. "I had a good time," he says. For the barest of moments, his gaze tracks over my face before moving to the horizon.

Our upper arms still touch; each small bunch of muscle and faint movement as he continues to twirl his keyring around his fingers sends an awareness through me. We sit like this for quite some time, until I get uncomfortable and decide to lean back on my forearms. The grittiness of the sand prickles my skin, but it gives my back a small respite.

In this position, Hayes is now higher than me, and the movement draws his gaze down to my level. "Do you want to sit between my legs? Prop your back against my chest? If I'd have known we'd be doing this, I would've brought fold-up chairs," he explains. Hayes mentions this as though it's the most natural thing to ask someone you only just met — and who also fell into bed, and couch, and car with your best friend — to get cozy with you on the beach.

Despite what I am beginning to wonder about the unique friendship between Trenton and Hayes, his offer sounds amazing; I'm already beginning to feel the strain in my shoulders from the way they are tweaked to recline. "Sure," I respond, crunching up and dusting the sand off my arms.

Hayes leans to the side and extends his leg slightly so he can gain access to his front pocket and shove his keys in there. Then, he pulls at the thighs of his jeans to straighten them as he positions his legs, knees, and feet just so, keeping his upper body propped up by resting back on his palms.

I stand, walk to between his legs, turn, sit down, and adjust. Once my elbows and arms are resting on his upper thighs and my hands are clasped together, I finally stop wiggling and relax.

He inhales and my head rises and falls on top of his chest with the motion. "Comfortable?" he asks with a slight hitch to the word.

"Very." Too comfortable. "You?"

His ab muscles flex against my back as he adjusts slightly. "Mm-hmm," he answers after a beat.

Unconvinced, I crank my neck to the side and look up at him over my shoulder. He peers down his nose at me, chin drawn back. "What?" he asks.

I press my lips together to contain a giggle. "Nothing. If you get uncomfortable, just let me know." Something tells me he's perpetually uncomfortable. Kinda makes me want to screw with him. Like… I don't know… maybe wiggle a little more, feigning an effort to adjust, while quite intentionally seeing just how uncomfortable I can actually make him.

I return my focus back to the sun, which now touches the horizon, and scoot my butt back against him ever so slightly.

His entire torso hardens and stops moving completely. Not even his chest rises or falls with the motion of breathing. He is, quite literally, holding his breath. It takes every bit of effort to not laugh.

When I settle again, the top of my hair moves faintly. Such a thing could easily be mistaken by the beach breeze, except this is warmer and steadier — the release of a carefully controlled breath.

Unfortunately, my trick backfires as that same breath travels down the side of my neck and resulting goosebumps cover my arms. My eyes widen as I mentally will them down, lest he see them and piece together how he'd managed to procure those bumps with a simple exhale.

Too late.

Hayes lets out a chuckle, trying to cover it up by clearing his throat. I unclasp my hands and squeeze his thighs between my fingers and thumbs. He jerks beneath me, and now it's my turn to laugh.

However, my laugh fades when the result of our teasing presses against my back. Pretending I don't feel his erection, I clasp my hands over my chest again and rest my head against him, just like when we first attempted this.

For the second time since we've been hanging out today, guilt seeps into the otherwise pleasant moment, wringing my insides like an oversaturated cloth. Maybe hanging out with my one-night stand's best friend and roommate wasn't a good idea after all. I move to sit up straight, when a young, feminine voice calls out his name from a ways farther from the shore.

The two of us separate like a shock of electricity, and we both scramble to stand, dusting sand off our clothes as we do.

"Hey, Hayes. One all meat and two everythings?" The pizza delivery driver is a girl. Young. Super cute. Beautiful even.

"Hey." Hayes steps up to her and pulls out his wallet, digging inside for…

Is that a twenty?

Didn't he pay with his credit card over the phone already?

He hands her the cash while she passes over the pizza boxes. A small smile graces her lips as she looks down at the twenty before tucking it away in her pocket. "Thanks." She starts to turn around but changes her mind and pauses. "How has Nikki been? God, it's been ages since I saw her last."

Hayes rubs the back of his neck and switches his weight from right foot to left. "Got the hell out of here as soon as she graduated."

Lainie nods, lets out a deep breath, and smiles. "Good for her."

"Yeah." Hayes clears his throat and drops his hand.

"Okay... well... you two enjoy. Predicted to be a sailor's sunset tonight — should be beautiful." She turns, waves over her shoulder, and tromps back through the sand.

Hayes returns to our spot, sits, and places the pizzas on his lap to protect them from the sandy ground. This, of course, leaves me to sit solo on the sand beside him again. An absolution I believe we are both unexpectedly thankful for.

The two of us continue watching the sun dip below the horizon. It takes all of about two minutes for it to hide completely and another short few before the colors begin transforming into pastels followed by bold pinks and oranges.

Watching the sunset never gets old; it's one of those sights that no matter where in the world you are, nor what your situation is, you can appreciate the simplistic beauty and moment. Life seems to stop for a few heartbeats, and the only thing existing is the painted sky. All you have to do is stop and pay attention.

Thanks to a slight breeze, the heady scent of bread and spices intermingles with the unmistakable, familiar scent of the salty gulf.

Once the bold colors in the sky take on a darker hue, Hayes stands. Propping the pizzas up on his hip, he holds out his hand. I readily accept, and he launches me forward and up.

When I am fully upright and he lets go of my hand, his fingertips drag along my palm and his eyes meet mine. Not usually one to shy away from a look like that, I lock gazes with him while dusting the sand off everywhere.

A gust of wind pushes through my hair, throwing strands across my eyes. When I move to brush them back behind my ear, our hands bump. His fingers drift over the tender part of my cheek as he tucks the strands, his gaze following a path from the bruise, to my mouth, and ending at my eyes.

"What *really* happened to your cheek?" he asks, eating up the already small bit of space between us with a step forward.

I take in a steadying breath and remind myself that liars blink and drop eye contact. My hand lifts, and I drag my fingers over the top of his. "I tried to cover it up," I whisper.

"Yeah, I know. That isn't what I asked you, though."

A hard swallow temporarily replaces a response. Hayes might be awkward, but that awkwardness lends to the fact that he is incredibly smart and perceptive. His thumb runs over the spot, similar to how Trenton's did last night.

"Like I said this morning: a bike accident," I rush out. "If you're worried that it was Trenton—"

Hayes bends his head down and presses his lips against mine, cutting off the words entirely. But he doesn't deepen the kiss — even when my body sways forward, proving I'd been more interested in him than I consciously allowed myself to believe today.

Instead, he drags his lips against mine and says, "I'd like to think that if Trenton did it, you wouldn't still be wearing the string he wrapped around your finger. Let me know when you change your mind and decide to tell us the truth."

There's somewhat of a threat in the comment. A threat toward what — who — left the mark on my cheek.

A tent of dread pitches over me, and I disappear beneath it. My head shakes and feet stumble backward.

Such a perfect day.

Almost.

In the absolute least, that kiss and my reception of it proves I'm in way over my head and not at all cut out for this life. The lies, deceit, and cunning. All the things Dad tried to shelter me from. The things I learned anyway, but never had to apply.

Until now.

CHAPTER TWENTY-ONE

"I bring sustenance!" I announce, entering the kitchen with pizzas in hand. Just in time, too, as Jude and Porter are digging through the pantry and fridge looking for their evening meal.

They don't even have the sense to ask where I'd been all day or how I managed to get pizza without a vehicle. All they care about is food. Now.

When we're all seated around the island, Porter asks the dreaded question, "So, how's the job going?"

I cast a glance at Jude, my much-more-patient brother, who is more like Dad in that he wouldn't ask unless time was short. "Answers come to those who are patient and don't press," he would always say. Unfortunately, answers also come to those who aren't patient nor willing to wait. The difference is that they are anxious in the meantime, always on edge, even volatile on occasion.

That's Porter in the present moment. "Find anything for us? You've been awful busy the past couple days." He leans forward on his elbows.

I twist open a bottle of ranch dressing, pour a good-sized glob onto my plate, pick up my fork, and cut off a chunk of my pizza slice. "Not since last time I gave an update. It'll take more than a twenty-four-hour period to get the information you want. I'm not going in, nitrous spraying." Chuckling, I take a moment to appreciate my tweak of 'guns blazing'. "Successful takeovers start with the element of surprise. Business Tactics 101. Right?"

Jude laughs around a man-sized bite, and Porter shoots him a glare. "What?" Jude chortles, placing his pizza down and leaning back in his chair, hands behind his head as he shrugs his shoulder and grins at his longtime friend. "She fucking sounds like Dad; it's hilarious." There's a spark of amusement in Jude's eyes but a flicker of sadness there, too.

I place the ranch-drenched piece of pizza in my mouth, then give them both a food-filled grin — something else Dad would have done. But then I turn my gaze on Porter, emboldened with Jude by my side. "I intend to follow through with the job. A little trust would be nice."

Since you're fucking me, in more ways than one, behind my brother's back.

Yes, I am bitter about it. Yes, I realize I should put a stop to this before things get too carried away. But that moroseness in Jude's eyes…

As though Porter can read my mind, he temples his fingers at his mouth, pizza forgotten, and bores a hard, cold glare at me, jaw moving over clenched teeth and a single eyebrow raised.

I swallow my bite before it's chewed enough, and the piece aches going down. My next words come out as a whisper as I recover and clear my throat. "I definitely found a group of car guys but don't yet have enough proof that they are associated with the specific racing club you're looking for." The pizza is still stuck, so I snatch my water bottle off the counter and take a big gulp. "Vehicle fanatics are a dime a dozen. The lead I found could be just a wannabe group who likes underglow kits, spinning rims, and sound systems."

Porter leans back and the space around the island instantly expands. Jude watches the two of us closely, listening for all the between-the-lines stuff like Dad always did.

"Well…" Porter props a knee up on one of the stool's crossbars and opens his legs loosely. "What is your next step?" he asks, trying, and failing, to sound nonchalant.

"The fuck, Porter? Give her a chance for Christ's sake," Jude finally pipes in.

"You've seen the books." Porter shrugs.

Jude presses his lips together and darts a cautious glance at me.

I get out of my stool abruptly. "This charade only just started!" I lash out. "Where's the money going that we've gone from taking steps to now being desperate?"

Jude might be my senior, my rock, but he withers under the accusation. Which, of course, immediately makes me feel horrible. I'm not accusing him of anything.

Porter keeps his douchbaginess en pointe with, "Hey, you're the one that refused to do any bookkeeping. Maybe if you actually involved yourself, these things wouldn't come as a surprise."

The doorbell rings, pulling all our attentions away from the unruly conversation. Jude hops down, collects my plate along with his, and heads to the garbage can. "Porter and I invited a few people over. Break the bread before doing business together sort of deal. We'll be downstairs if you want to make an appearance."

Porter's eyes spark in amusement.

Which undoubtedly means women are involved.

Is he looking for a flash of jealousy?

Anger?

Go… go fuck them.

Gives me a damn break at least.

Just wrap it up, bruh.

CHAPTER TWENTY-TWO

Trenton

The creak of the front door opening gives me enough reason to shoot out of bed. I'd been struggling to sleep anyway; it didn't matter how many times I switched sides or how I positioned the pillows, sleep was being an elusive bastard.

Hayes left with Remi this morning and is only just now getting back... after midnight? Since she is the very reason I can't sleep anyway, I slip into my sweats and leave the room before Hayes has time to hide away in his.

He stops dead, a deer-in-the-headlights look on his face when I appear. "What are you still doing awake?" he asks, knowing in the rare occurrence that I have a day off, I tend to pass out early.

"Why are you only just now getting home?" I scrutinize back.

The two of us burst into laughter.

"Okay, Mom... sorry I worried you." Hayes tosses his keys into the junk bowl on the bartop and goes straight to the fridge.

Truth is, it's not so much that he worried me; it's the fact that Remi did something to my mind and body, and he was gone all day after spending time with her.

Not jealousy. Not with Hayes. At least I don't think. But... I don't know. Fucking something.

I try to hold off — patience and all — but the question bursts out of me prematurely anyway. Ironically not at all unlike my budding obsession with the minx. "How'd the ride with Remi go today?" Hayes pulls out a beer. A fucking beer. Crow and I are the more frequent drinkers... not him. And definitely not at home in the middle of the night. I lean against the counter and cross my arms, fingers gripping the shirt at my sides where he can't see them. "That good, hm?"

"Something is up with the mark on her cheek," he says, twisting the cap off on his forearm. A heavy weight presses on my chest. I had thought the same thing. Hayes has a history with that sort of stuff, though — him having a father of the year and all that. He can hone in on foul play pretty easy. "Hurt watching her lie about it. So... I kissed her. Tried to catch her off guard for a minute. See if she would say something."

Fuck. I drop my arms, move to the fridge, and take out a beer to join him. "You good, man?"

Hayes sighs and he takes another pull, opposite fingers tapping on his thigh. "She had me drop her off at a corner store so she could go take a shower. When she got back, she was still wearing the string ring you made."

My heart skips a beat at hearing that. The obvious thing to do, of course, is ignore the comment, open my beer, and take a swig.

"Wanna tell me what that was all about?" he presses.

I turn around, open the fridge, grab a second beer, and hold it up. "That's a double fister, bro. Really want to go there?"

He laughs, and I put the prop back with a groan.

"That good, hm?" he says, mocking my earlier comment.

"Yeah... that damn good."

A silence falls between us. An unusual one that twists my insides. We share a look and both take another drink at the same time.

"She the reason you can't go to sleep?" he asks.

"She the reason you're drinking a beer at midnight?" I return.

Hayes lifts his bottle, tilting the neck toward me. I meet him halfway. The glass tinks in the quiet house.

Silence descends again. As quiet as he is around women, I am usually an exception to that rule. Thankfully, tonight is no different. "The ride went well," he starts. Really fucking well if the tapping of his fingers on his thigh are any indicator.

My mind wars with how I am supposed to feel about this. Hayes and I both know how to fuck women. But that's the long and short of it. Neither of us commit to anything more than bringing them to bed. Never have. Not even in high school. There's too much fun to be had, after all.

"She knows how to drive a stick."

"Damn straight she does!"

We laugh.

Wait... "Hang on. You let her drive? So... what... you're going to antagonize me for a string ring, but let her behind the wheel of your baby?" I hold my hand up and curl my fingers inward. "Zero. That's the number of times you've let anyone drive your car. Me included."

Hayes takes another drink, finishing the bottle, and gets out another, immediately popping the top. I lift an eyebrow. He narrows a glare at me down the length of the bottle as he takes another pull.

My stomach becomes leaden. This doesn't have anything to do with Remi specifically. It has everything to do with the mark on her cheek. Demons have come back to haunt him in mottled shades of red and midnight-blue on the face of a pretty girl.

"Is that jealousy I hear?" He grins, but the smile fades. "I didn't let her behind the wheel. Just let her shift."

A small amount of breath vents out of me, and my shoulders release a bit of tension with the exhale.

Am I relieved?

Hell if I fucking know.

Maybe.

Hayes shoves his hand into his pocket, beer gripped at his stomach. "Hey, you good?" he asks, putting a clarity to what I thought was maybe a coincidence. "It was just a ride."

"Yeah." I rub the back of my neck. "Same here. Just a ride." I tick my mouth up in a half grin.

Hayes shakes his head and laughs. But that tension returns, so now it's my turn to ask. "Need me to back off?" He is my best friend. Fuck, she did something to me, but that doesn't trump years of friendship.

"Are you serious?" The beer is settling, and his words come out slightly slurred.

Light weight.

When I don't respond with a joke or quip, his eyes widen. "You claimed her immediately. I was just an innocent bystander. All good." He takes another long pull.

I can't help but chuckle. "Oh ho ho ho. No you're not." Hayes has this weird intuition radar, and apparently she sets it off as easily as she sets off my fuck radar.

He rolls his eyes at me and finishes off his beer. "I'm calling it a night."

A laugh bursts out of me. "You're not going to sleep."

"Nope," he says with a laugh of his own as he leaves the kitchen. "Bets down that you aren't either."

"Hm, not betting on something that is a guaranteed loss."

He chuckles once more, and his bedroom door closes with a click. I dump the rest of my beer out, really having only picked it up to support Hayes, and rub my hands down my face.

I fucking can't get her out of my head. Both heads. I peer down at my growing cock at the thought. With a growl of frustration, I make my way back to my room.

CHAPTER TWENTY-THREE

Remi

I quickly learn the sound barriers in this house are lacking. High-pitched female giggles and the low hum of male speech filters through the office room floor. The gathering started early and doesn't seem to have an end in sight. This was much more than a breaking of bread. This was an initiation. The building of a group.

While I try to find the race club, Porter and Jude begin the foundations of their own. They are trying to recruit the numbers that should give them enough sway to initiate a takeover when the time is right.

The vibrating buzz of my phone against the office desk has me finally removing my gaze from the computer screen. It's almost one in the morning and I am exhausted, but there are far too many thoughts running through my mind for sleep to come. Doing more research seemed like a good idea.

As for the text, my guess is Porter's piece of ass isn't giving it up, and he's checking to see if I'm awake and ready for a romp. Wanting to see if the woman who always gives it up is available.

:Trenton: Get out of my head. Sleep would be nice.

An unexpected snort-laugh emits from my nose. When he sees that I am online, flashing dots immediately appear.

:Trenton: Please tell me you're not one of those people who keep their sound notifications on all night even when they're sleeping. Because I texted to grovel. If I woke you up, that means double groveling.

:Me: Grovel?

I wrack my mind trying to figure out why he would feel a need to apologize for anything that wasn't mutual.

:Trenton: Passing you off on Hayes instead of taking you home myself. Holding your clothes hostage. Let me make it up to you? Crowbar, take two. Friday night at restaurant closing. There's somewhere I want to take you. Plus, I'd really like my clothes back... those are my favorite workout shorts after all.

The laughter he so easily pulls from me fills the quiet room, and I grimace at the echoey sound.

:Me: *What about my clothes? Do I get those back?*

:Trenton: *Most of them ;)*

:Me: *Oh jeez. Perv. Okay, well, speaking of clothes, what type am I expected to wear Friday?*

:Trenton: *The ones you were wearing when we got out of my car.*

:Me: *Funny. Very funny.*

:Trenton: *Something sexy, but comfortable?*

:Me: *Hmm… I might be able to manage that.*

Dots appear and disappear and reappear. I watch in anticipation as he composes his next message. Funny how little flashing dots can send a spear of want straight to between my thighs. My mind replays the last text messages we had sent and the end result. Anytime I'm idle, last night together is exactly where my mind decides to settle.

Even so, I am still surprised that I'm getting a text back. At least this soon. The sex was amazing — more than amazing — but we'd mutually agreed for something casual. I immediately wanted more. I would be lying to myself if I admitted anything otherwise.

The chime of my ringtone pairs with the vibration, and my fingers immediately rush to the volume button as I dart a panicked glance at the floor. The concern of Porter hearing my phone go off in the middle of the night is irrational with the party going strong, but it is still an unfortunate knee-jerk reaction.

I stare down as Trenton's name flashes across the screen. I swipe the connect button and place the phone to my ear. "Hey," I whisper, still worried about being heard.

"Hey," Trenton whispers back, and his deepened timbre rolls through me. "Friday is a long time from now. I wanted to hear your voice," he explains.

A woman's high-pitched squeal rings throughout the house, and I quickly cover the speaker with my palm. Shit.

Trenton is quiet for only a moment before piecing things together. "Ah, you have people over. Sorry, I should have asked first."

"No… it's fine. My brother and our roommate have some new friends visiting. I'm hiding."

"Why aren't you hanging out with them and having a good time?"

I take in a deep breath and exhale. "Needed to take care of some transition stuff. Look up a few things."

"In the middle of the night?"

"What's your excuse?" Leaning back in the office chair, I ask with a chuckle.

"You," he answers. "The way your stomach trembles beneath my fingers. The sigh you let out after every orgasm. The way you say my name and roll your hips."

Studying the string around my finger, I respond breathlessly, "Friday is a long time from now."

"Mm, I agree. I know you're dying to get me in bed again, but I had something else in mind for Friday."

"Oh?"

"A night out. Not one in. You know, like a proper—" A muffled knock crosses the line, cutting Trenton's comment short.

"Sounds like you have someone over, too," I point out, feeling the weight of disappointment sink in my stomach.

Trenton laughs. "The only person who would knock on my door at this time would be Hayes. Seems you're keeping him up, too." The turn of a handle and slight creak of his bedroom door opening can be heard in the background.

A sudden underproduction of saliva turns my throat dry.

What did Hayes tell Trenton about our day together?

150

It shouldn't matter. Trenton and I had an agreement. The fact that even mere texts with the man makes me throb with need doesn't discount the fact that what we did was meant to be fun — a one-time thing.

There isn't a rule that says it's wrong for me to create connections with someone else. I guess maybe because it is his friend that makes it a little... weird? Against the rules?

"Rumor has it, you two had a good time together?" Trenton asks nonchalantly, the click and hum of the line tells me he put our call on speaker.

I prop my phone against my shoulder and twist my fingers in my lap. "Well, I can't speak for Hayes, but I had a good time. Really appreciated the tour of the area. Watching the sunset was a nice touch, too."

"Hayes showing me up, as usual." Trenton's voice changes as he pulls back from the phone and directs the next part of the conversation toward Hayes. "I invited her to meet me at The Crowbar Friday night after my shift."

The rustle of something comes across the line, and Hayes speaks up. "Since Trenton is working, do you want me to come pick you up?" he asks.

Trenton groans, and the sound of a smack echoes between the lines. "See what I mean? Always the knight in shining armor. Can't catch a break with this guy."

Both of them have such a smooth way of making me feel light and happy. A giddiness for an entirely different reason makes my heart flip, though, and a smirk pulls at my lips. "No, not this time. I can just take my bike."

The line goes silent, and muffled whisperings meet my ear. Trenton returns to our conversation first. "So, Hayes and I want to extend an invitation of hospitality to you. If you ever need a place to hang out day or night, give one of us a call or shoot us a text. Even if I'm at The Crowbar. Hayes is usually here working from home."

That giddy feeling from a moment ago inflates but deflates right away. A number of conflicted thoughts and emotions go through me at the same time. If it weren't for him mentioning that I could come over even if he wasn't home, I would have thought it was just an open invitation for a booty call.

The primary reaction winning over in my heart and mind, however, is the fact that I wish I could take them up on that offer. Every day and night for a while, or at least until I have gotten to the bottom of this car racing shit and have something more solid to give Jude and Porter. Because then maybe when I come back, Porter won't breathe down my neck so much. How amazing it would be to tell them I'm staying at a friend's house on occasion. To be away from the constant reminder of how drastically different my world is now in comparison to just a few months ago.

"Too ballsy?" Trenton asks, his voice low. I had gone too long without responding. Really, I'd love nothing more than to get on my bike and head over there now, if I'm being honest. Friday is a long ways away. A long time to go without getting information, too, especially with how impatient Porter is being. My chest tightens at the thought that I'll be stuck here day in and day out in the meantime.

Questions suddenly claw at my throat, demanding to be let free.

Hey, do you know about an underground racing club?

Can you give me a name?

Help me!

"No…" I say on an exhale. "I wish I could take you up on that offer. I just don't think that would be a good idea."

God if that doesn't leave a million questions floating between us.

Why?

Why isn't it a good idea?

Every potential excuse I can think of seems pathetic.

I could say something along the lines of wanting to make sure I am here to support Jude because we just lost our father, but I'm not ready to reveal that bit of my recent past yet. And I certainly don't want to mention Porter's new-found appreciation for harassment. Nor do I want to risk his wrath and have things revealed that would be better left tightly packaged should I screw up. I don't want to throw so many red flags that these guys stop trusting me, and rumor gets around that someone is seeking information and they end up locking it up even tighter than it already is.

Just thinking about it all is exhausting.

"Okay." There's patience and the hint of a smile woven in Trenton's tone. "No strings attached," he adds. But of course my eyes flit down to the string around my finger and a quiet chuckle escapes me.

CHAPTER TWENTY-FOUR

T hree long days go by. Hours upon hours are spent on the computer trying to find more information in some of the local forums. When Porter pries, I escape on my bike under the ruse of checking another potential meetup location. It isn't always a ruse; I do try to hit up areas with long stretches of road, desolate spots, or straight freeway sections during low-traffic times. It also gives me opportunities to look for things like skid marks or speed traps. Then, I get back late enough so he doesn't pester me. It seems effective. Jude and Porter's busy work increases, though, which also aids in keeping them distracted.

Every night, Trenton and Hayes text me to ask me how my day went. The answer is usually the same: job searching online, getting used to the area, things like that. The truth, yet not the entire truth. Before I go to sleep each night, Trenton sends me a countdown reminding me of our "date." Hayes, on the other hand, usually keeps the check-in pretty basic.

I keep waiting each day for Trenton to skip the text because he has some fun over for the evening. That isn't the case; he never forgets. Never misses an opportunity to touch base.

Thursday night rolls around, and the anticipation becomes nearly unbearable. Seeing as it was exactly a week ago I found the odd forum post about The Crowbar, I stalk the forum all day, curiously wondering if this "date" at The Crowbar coincides with another meetup like last week.

Much to my excitement, it does end up being the case. Apparently, I'm not too shabby at sleuthing after all. Plus, the more I interact with Hayes and Trenton, the more conviction I feel that they're somehow involved in this elusive street racing circle; they are car guys and proud of their vehicles, but they keep the car-related discussions to a minimum even after having learned that I know a thing or two. In a lot of ways, their silence is louder than their open discussion would be. But that silence doesn't provide me with solid proof.

Just like a week ago, the profile with a crow avatar — who I now assume is Crow himself — writes a vague post.

:grub11close:

So, they have something planned at the restaurant at close again. This time, on the eleventh.

Tomorrow.

Last week, I learned the hard way to keep my forum profile status set to offline. And again about midweek when I forgot to set it as invisible before popping on. Car forum members are like a moth to a flame when a female avatar and name pops up as online. I can hardly scroll the forum without a chat bubble popping up.

The one time I did make that mistake, Hayes offered assistance again. That time, I spotted the admin badge near his name. Before changing my status as offline, I sent him a quick "pew, pew" just for kicks. As far as I know, he isn't aware that DoubleD is me, but he still played along, sending back one of those gun emojis.

I couldn't wipe the grin off my face.

Conversations with Hayes have steadily gotten longer throughout the week, too. Instead of one- or two-word responses, he is now being a bit more talkative with his texts — somewhere along the four- or five-word response mark.

Progress.

He's a nerd, not a mute. My money is on that he is plenty chatty, but it takes being part of his circle to earn that reward. Part of me wants inside that circle. To hear what he has to say. To be someone he wants to talk to.

Amid witty text banter and daily updates, friendships seem to have formed. Trenton has continued to text me while not mentioning our one-night thing and not pushing to have a repeat. The seemingly legit and continued, casual interest is about as much of a turn on as the immediate physical interest was.

My stomach flips at the thought of seeing them both again, bringing me right back to the days in high school when that anticipation made your fingers shaky and caused funny sensations to swirl in your belly.

When the time finally rolls around that I need to get dressed and ready to go, I quite intentionally pick out a pair of shorts like the ones I wore to The Crowbar that first night. I usually prefer jeans when riding, but tonight I intend on making a statement. These guys may think they are getting to know me, but once they see what I ride, their entire perceptions are bound to change. It's not a secret I really planned to keep, but after a bit, I decided it would be a fun surprise.

Add in a sexy outfit, and the first impression should be epic. There's a lot I've been looking forward to about this night all week. Seeing them tops the list, but the more I've gotten to know them, having them see me… a peek at the real me… the more exciting this element has become.

Nerves course through me, too. Will they be frustrated that I didn't tell them? Will they be disappointed in my vehicle? Not that it really matters, but apparently they've somehow made me care about their opinions.

Damn them.

The difference in tonight's outfit of choice is that I don't intend on wearing light colors like I did that first night. Black, all the way. The cutoffs are black, the white dangling torn strings clashing against my tanned upper thighs. My shirt is pure black, too, short enough to show just the right amount of lower stomach, tight enough not to fly up while riding.

Trenton said comfortable. I won't be comfortable with these clothes while riding, but as soon as I get off, I should be fine.

I twist my hair up and secure it with a small clip — one that's easy to remove once my helmet is off.

The trickiest part is that I want to intentionally show up late. Not before Trenton gets off work like last time, but afterward, once the other cars start arriving.

One hundred percent ready, the plastic bag of Trenton's clothes and a compact-sized clutch purse for essentials like my license and a bit of cash in hand, I leave my room and plop onto the couch across from the unused fireplace, throwing my head back against the cushions. My knee bounces as the minutes crawl by.

"So… who is the lucky fucker?" Porter's voice has me nearly flying off the couch.

Whipping my head around, I peer over my shoulder toward the dark kitchen. "Holy fuck, Porter! We have lights, you know?"

"Come here," he says. Or, rather demands. I turn my head back toward the fireplace wishing there were flames that could aid in my excuse for not standing up on his command. "Don't fucking piss me off, Remi," he warns.

Stomach and heart clashing, I stand up and make my way over to the kitchen. He's leaning against the island, hands in his pockets. I walk right up to him and lift my gaze to look up in his eyes.

Perhaps emboldened by the fact that I am about to leave, or maybe it is because he hasn't bothered me for a good part of a few days, I say, "What changed with you? You were never like this before." My voice isn't nearly as strong as I would have liked, but at least the thought is out there.

Porter smirks and gives a light chuckle, removing his hands from his pockets where I was certain just moments ago they would stay.

His fingers and thumb come to my face, gripping my jaw. His eyes track from mine down to my mouth. Instead of moving back up again, though, they lock there and his tongue slips out to wet his lips. "You know… that innocence… that naivety… is what has always fucking turned me on." His other hand slides between my legs. "I've always been like this; you were just too stupid to see it. Too young. But now that I can fucking take you when and where I want… and you're still so fucking gullible…"

160

His hand slips into my shorts, further simplified by the fact that I've chosen to not wear underwear. Trenton was right — access is so much easier this way. Too easy. Porter groans and thrusts three, thick fingers inside me. No warming me up, no lubricating dip, he just drives them in.

Tears prick my eyes. I've never cried in front of him about his mistreatment. But this time, my tears betray me. Little sparks of fire track down my cheeks.

"I asked you a question, Remi."

Too overwhelmed as he plunges in and out and his opposite fingers bite my jaw, collecting the wetness, I'd forgotten he had asked a question. He shoves harder, knuckles bruising against my sex. The breath is knocked out of my lungs. I blink to clear my vision.

In this moment, I realize this is my fault.

I've never actually given him reason or told him to stop.

"Stop," I whimper, trying defense on for size.

Porter freezes. His expression goes from stunned to pure rage. But he pulls out of me. My spine immediately curves in on itself, and a heavy breath whooshes from my lungs. I hadn't meant to outwardly display my relief, but my body did it anyway.

Porter's fingers leave my jaw. In the next second those same fingers lift and fall against the side of my face, knuckle side down. My eyes water for an entirely different reason this time. He had hit the same side that was nearly almost healed, but the buried tenderness now blazes back to life.

"And, see, all these years I had hoped you'd know better once you became old enough to have some fucking sense." He lifts the hand he'd been fingering me with and wraps his tongue around every digit. "Now, answer my fucking question."

My mind works in overtime, rewinding on super speed as I try to remember what he had asked. I came out here, sat down…

Who is the lucky fucker?

I was sitting on the couch, alone. What is he talking about? My eyebrows curve inward and I hate that I have to silently plead with him. Without words I have to beg him to repeat the question. To explain. Because apparently he's right; apparently I don't have any sense.

He pushes me away from him, disgust creasing his features. "This hot number." He gestures to my outfit. "It makes me want to bend you over against this damn island and shove my cock inside you so deep you go blind. Who the fuck are you wearing it for?"

Trenton.

Hayes.

Whoever will look at me and actually appreciate it.

For fun.

For attention.

162

Not this kind of attention.

"Another lead. I have a feeling this one is the real deal," I say much steadier than I anticipated. But even so, I instantly regret revealing that information. My body, mind, and soul know it's what he wants to hear, though. "Figured a little show of skin would get me answers faster."

Porter crosses his arms and feet and leans against the island again. "Go clean up your face then and get the hell out of here before I fucking do something to make you late."

I don't dawdle. In an instant, I am around the bar, darting down the hallway and into my room and bathroom.

Red blooms on my cheek. The light amount of mascara on my lashes didn't quite have enough time to dry all the way, and little flecks and smears line my face.

My fingers grip the sink counter hard as sadness and fear are replaced with anger. I crank the cold water on high, rinse my face, sling my vanity mirror open, and get out my concealer to quickly dab on the slightly greenish tinted cream.

CHAPTER TWENTY-FIVE

Crow

"I'm blaming you because you're usually the problem." Trenton glares at me, popping his trunk and lugging out a cooler.

"Whatever makes you feel better." I shrug and take over, pulling the handle up and wheeling it to the front of the restaurant. His piece of ass that has him all self cock-blocked hasn't shown up yet, and damn he's been talking about her since that day she walked into the bar.

Hayes laughs, "Makes sense. Last time she was here, you walked in and she couldn't leave fast enough." He rubs his chest as if the memory of her running into him is still fresh. "She's probably thinking, 'Damn that emo guy might show up again, better not go after all.'"

I position the cooler against the front outside wall where everyone is starting to gather, unhook the lid, and shove my hand into the ice to the very bottom for the coldest bottle. When I take it out, I turn to Hayes, bat my eyelashes, and hand it to him. "Do me a solid, and open this for me."

Hayes rolls his eyes but takes the bottle and twists off the top with his forearm. For as little as he drinks, he's always the one showing us up. Hell, get him a can and the fucker can shotgun like a whore whose specialty is sucking multiple cocks at once.

As usual, he doesn't drink tonight. Even when I take out a second and try to hand it to him. He waves it off, so I toss it to a random crew leader.

Something has the guy and his group of member-initiates' attention glued toward the street. Going on guard, I follow their line of sight. The reverberation of a motorcycle meets my ears before the bike and its owner come into view, though. The unique rattle of a dry clutch and the deep bass precedes the sight.

Those sounds aren't well known; they're different, which is why the majority of attendees have stopped talking and their eyes are now on the road as the Duc leans into the turn at the entrance to the parking lot.

Once the onlookers' amazement moves past the sound, the surprises don't end there. Beer now forgotten, hanging loose between my hooked forefinger and thumb, my eyes hone in on the legs and thighs that wrap over the seat.

Call me fucking crazy, but see them once, and there's no mistaking who they belong to. "I thought you said she rode a fucking bicycle," I whisper under my breath to Hayes.

Hayes chokes over a cough, his hand coming to his mouth to cover the sound. "I said she was headed toward the bike rack."

Trenton is bug-eyed watching as this girl he's been obsessing over stops right in front of us and balances the bike between her legs like a pro. "A Duc… she drives a fucking Duc and you didn't tell me?" he gasps. "No wonder she was bruised up from a bike ride!" Trenton tries to keep his voice to a whisper, but there's panic and venom there.

"Hey, I didn't know! She rode here that first night on an actual bicycle… with pedals. And I still stand by my opinion that that bruise didn't come from riding."

Bruise?

I turn to ask what the hell they're talking about, but she pops the kickstand and lifts her leg to sling it over the seat. All of our gazes follow the inner line of her legs all the way to the apex where her short-ass shorts sure as hell don't leave anything to the imagination.

To top it off… she's wearing all black.

Even her bike is black — naked.

That's actually what pulls me out of my trance. I elbow Trenton in the side as she removes her matte-black helmet, hooks it to the bike, then takes a clip out of her hair. Black hair falls long and slightly wavy against her just-as-black shirt.

166

Everything that's usually my type, not his.

I don't even have to open my mouth to elaborate why I'm elbowing him. He snaps a glare and hilarious scowl in my direction.

Kid-fucking-not, she shakes her head side to side before running her fingers through the top to fix what the helmet messed up. Once that's taken care of, she opens up a small side case cargo rack, pulls out her cellphone, slides it into her back pocket — the one that literally comes out of the bottom of her shorts. It's somewhat dark out here aside from the parking lot lights and headlights, but I am fairly certain that is a line of ass cheek just beneath it.

She then wrangles out a tightly-fit plastic bag before locking up.

I lower my beer, resting it by my zipper as casually as possible. Hayes and Trenton stand gaping and blinking like they're opening a porn mag spread for the first time.

Look away, Crow. Look away.

But I can't. When she finally takes in her surroundings, finds us, and her eyes land on me, my cock twitches, and I'm half tempted to grab Hayes by the shoulders and pull him in front of me.

She walks forward, her attention switching between the three of us and a smile lifting up the corner of her lips.

Trenton grasps his chest, turning on the dramatics instantly. Hayes swallows hard, curling into his awkward shell. I lean back against the brick wall and take a swig of my beer before dropping my gaze to the concrete.

Her black sneakers enter my peripheral as she steps up close to Hayes and their bodies connect. In a hug, I assume, but I can't bring myself to look up. When her feet step in front of me, my lungs constrict, trying to suffocate me.

"Don't be rude, Crow," Trenton says.

I wrench my gaze off the ground and meet hers. Fucking sparks or some shit erupt between us. If I could back up more I would, but the brick wall won't move. Since I can only assume that they were doing introductions, I tilt my beer at her and say, "Nice to meet you." The bruise they had mentioned draws my attention to her cheek.

When Hayes laughs, I realize I'm screwed; I missed a signal somewhere. He introduces us, and the entire time he's going through the formalities — "Crow this is Remi; Remi this is Crow" — her dark-brown eyes are locked on mine like she's trying to deconstruct me or some shit.

I already said it was nice to meet her, so I don't say anything this time. My eyes drop to her chest, despite knowing that is not what you are supposed to do when you first officially meet a woman. But the way it rises and falls as she looks at me is fucking intoxicating.

"Do you drive the black Supra?" she asks, and that instantly persuades my focus back up to her face.

We're at a meetup; people asking what car you drive is not a big fucking deal. But for whatever reason, like an idiot, I give a pathetic nod.

Maybe I've been hanging out with Hayes for too long.

Honestly, the way she so easily gets under my skin and seeps into my bones, filling me with a more-than-unsettling warmth, irritates the hell out of me. "So, a Duc? Funny how these guys you've been stringing along didn't know you came from money."

She reels back, tucking her chin a bit, then lifts it and narrows her eyes on me again. I instantly regret saying anything to her at all. Whatever it takes to make sure we don't make eye contact. Because that obstinance — that tenacity — she exudes, makes me hard. "Bet you have more money under the hood than my bike costs off the lot. And we both know that in a stock race, mine would burn yours off the line."

I straighten. "Well no shit, sugar. Yours is a fucking motorcycle."

She clenches her teeth and gives me a tight grin.
Okay, so this didn't go over well.
Not at all.

So I don't piss my friends off more than I probably already have, I storm off and join another group. Didn't take me long to realize that she pushes all my buttons… in more ways than one.

Fucking trouble.

She's the type of girl that makes men stupid, and like hell am I going to fall into that category.

CHAPTER TWENTY-SIX

For a few heartbeats I just stand there staring at the brick wall where Crow just stood. I've been around the block enough times to instantly realize I was right about my initial opinion about him: he is every bit my type... right down to being an asshole.

A likable asshole.

Sur-fucking-prise.

My heart beats a mile a minute realizing that I also just screwed up my interaction with whom I assume is the leader of this club. And, based on what he said, there's a chance Trenton and Hayes might be upset as well.

That sure didn't play out as I had hoped.

I tentatively turn toward them. Hayes is now leaning against the wall. Trenton is glaring over his shoulder in Crow's direction.

"The car hauler came the day Hayes took me out," I admit, drawing both their attentions toward me. "Sorry I didn't tell you. I was looking forward to the element of surprise."

171

Trenton grins and hands Hayes his beer. "Oh, you definitely surprised us. Can't speak for Hayes here, but I never asked you what you drive."

Hayes shakes his head. "Nope, me neither."

"That's on us. Don't worry about Crow; he just doesn't do well with anything exciting and fun."

Yeah... I know his type. Dark and brooding. A bit rough. Usually in the best way.

Trenton steps forward, takes my left hand in his and slips his other hand around my lower back, tugging me in close. He lifts my knuckles to his mouth and gives them a light kiss. "Part of me is a little heartbroken that you hugged Hayes first." His thumb skims over the string ring and his eyes meet mine.

"He was the only one not holding a drink," I respond.

Plus, I don't know, it just seemed like the right thing to do at the time.

I hold up the plastic bag containing his clothes. Trenton steps back, takes the bag with one hand but keeps hold of my other hand, weaving our fingers together. My pulse stutters at the motion; we haven't seen each other since our first night together, much less touched. He was forward then, and he is being forward now, so it shouldn't come as much of a surprise.

What comes as more of a surprise, though, is that I like it. Our hands interwoven like it's the most natural thing.

My next swallow is harder as the punch of reality settles uneasy in the pit of my stomach.

I casually remove my hand from his and reach for my cell phone to make it appear as though I am responding to a message instead of avoiding the way his touch makes me feel.

My cheek stings at the memory of what happened right before I left the house and serves as a second-by-second reminder that the stakes have been raised. Whatever it is that's going on between Trenton, Hayes, and me is dangerous and detrimental to the underlying reason why I am here.

Well, one of the reasons. The main reason. Seems I keep needing to remind myself which reason is the more time sensitive and important one.

I open the text chat between Jude, Porter, and myself and begin to type details of this particular meetup, like the location and to let them know it's going on right now. But with a glance at the congregating vehicles, it still doesn't seem like anything more than peacocking. Hoods are open, drinks sloshing, engines revving; nobody here appears to be gearing up to race tonight. Plus, there are only about ten cars in attendance. I delete the few words I had typed, deciding against the idea.

When I pocket my phone and Trenton doesn't reach for my hand again, a puddle of disappointment mixed with relief pools in my gut.

He and Crow exchange a look. Trenton snags his beer back from Hayes and holds up a finger over his shoulder as he heads toward Crow.

Now alone with Hayes, I wave a hand at the cars and state, "Not that I hadn't already pegged it, but a car club, hm?"

Something has him wound up. One of his hands is shoved into a pocket, while the other is balled at his thigh.

I toy with the idea to ask him what's wrong, but figure we probably aren't on those kinds of terms just yet. Our friendly banter via text over the past week makes me want to reach out and touch him, though. Say something. Make him smile. I don't know.

Instead, I lean against the wall at his side, close enough that our shoulders touch like they did on the beach. He looks down at me and gives me a soft smile. "Yeah."

"Sounds fun. What type of club is it, and what sort of activities do they organize?" The cars aren't a specific make — they aren't all classics, supers, or restored vehicles.

Hayes's observations move to Crow and Trenton. Crow rubs his tattooed hand over his jaw and looks up at me from a downward tilted head in response to something Trenton is saying before moving his attention to Hayes.

The rev of a vehicle pulls his focus to the lot, and he drops his hand to the side, eyes seeking the source.

Following their lines of sight, my entire body turns rigid and blood rushes in a torrent down to my feet.

A red Mustang.

My mind screams, *"No! What is he doing here!?"*

My body steps ahead, putting distance between Hayes and me.

The 'Stang rolls forward, an arm hanging from the passenger window.

No...

No, no, no.

Once the vehicle is directly in front of me, I learn Porter is actually the passenger. Dipping my head down to look inside, Jude flashes me a grin.

I swallow hard and straighten. Porter's eyes flick over the scene, alighting on me for the briefest of moments. Ice freezes along my spine. That single look is all it takes to deliver his intended warning: He isn't looking at the vehicles in attendance; he's seeking out which guy it is that I dressed this way for. With a side-step, I successfully put enough distance between me and everyone else standing around.

My hands come to the hem of my shorts, and I grip the high material to tug it down before I realize what I am doing and loosen my fingers.

Do not cower.

Act normal.

Porter's continued perusal lands over my right shoulder. He displays one of his deceivingly friendly smiles and a prickle of air brushes against my skin as someone passes me.

Black jeans, black boots, and a black shirt that is taut against tattooed-covered biceps block my view. Crow approaches the passenger window and leans his elbows on the track.

"Well, well… What do we have here? You headed to the streets?" Porter's voice meets my ears.

"Sorry, wrong type of meetup, man. Feel free to park and show off a little, though," Crow responds, giving the top of the car a couple of firm pats.

Oh shit… no…

Please don't invite them to stay.

Hayes steps to my side, alternating a quick glance from me to the Mustang and back to me again as Jude circles around the lot, looking for an ideal spot. Why the hell he isn't driving his own car is beyond me. Thankfully, they park near the entrance, no doubt in case they want to make a quick exit.

Hayes and I are standing near the opposite end, which serves to relieve a bit of my anxiousness, but the feeling soon morphs into anger and frustration instead.

They gave me a job and here they are babysitting me?

What the actual fuck?

And how the hell did they know to come here?

When Jude meets my eyes for the first time from their parking spot, I quite openly share my annoyance with the press of my lips. Brother whom I love or not, this is not fucking okay.

Hayes eventually starts mulling around while I slink to the shadows against the wall and act all pensive and pissed off — not at all behaving the way I should be. But Jude and Porter arriving threw me for a loop. As it stands, whether or not I am cut out for what they've tasked me with is definitely questionable. But the blatant distrust in at least giving me free range to try…

Teeth snagging on the inside of my cheek, I narrow one last glare in their direction before grabbing my phone.

:Me: What the hell are you doing here? Thought I was on the payroll.

I give the message a few seconds for it to cross airwaves and watch as Jude digs his phone out of his pocket. His eyes seek the crowd until he finds me before flicking down to his screen and thumbing in a response.

:Jude: Porter said you gave him a location.

With a raised eyebrow, I quickly swipe-text him back.

:Me: Porter is full of shit.

Jude leans against the closed driver's door and commits to the back and forth while Porter talks to a guy who is looking under the hood.

:Jude: Want us gone?

:Me: Yep.

Just like that, Jude pockets his phone and approaches Porter. I quickly write one more text, hoping he'll get it before Porter stops talking to the guy ogling his car.

:Me: Hey... don't bring this up to Porter, okay? Just... give me a couple more days, then I'll give him an update myself.

Jude's eyes flick down, and he digs his phone out again. This time he doesn't bother to reply, he simply shoots me a look and quick head tilt.

CHAPTER TWENTY-SEVEN

"Hey, you alright?" Trenton's voice removes me from the distraction, and I quickly put my phone away.

"Hm? Oh… Yeah. Just been a while since I've attended a meetup is all. So much testosterone."

His gaze travels toward the red Mustang that has monopolized all my extra attention, head tilting to the side and eyebrows pinching inward.

I decide to turn the tables, trying to get my mind off Jude and Porter and back to the tasks at hand. To at least appear I am not wound up and stressed out. I dart a glance over his shoulder toward Hayes and ask, "I was actually wondering the same thing about Hayes. I know we haven't known each other for long, but… is he alright?"

Trenton blinks away whatever thoughts the Mustang had conjured and his lips stretch into a smile. "I'm sure he wouldn't be opposed to another hug," he says with a wink. But then the smile fades and he takes a step closer to me, eyes tracking over my face. He swallows hard and inhales deeply. "Did you get into another bicycle accident?" he asks, eyes going dark as they land on my cheek.

It takes every bit of willpower not to yell out "Fuck!" and ball my fists. With a frustrated exhale I shake my head. "No... why?"

"Because after a week, your cheek is worse, Remi," he chastises as if he has known me for longer than a week. When I don't respond, eyebrows flattening, he continues, "Your helmet wiped off the makeup."

Ugh, not surprising. That is one of the very reasons I seldom wear makeup to begin with. "I thought we were talking about Hayes," I point out, trying to redirect the topic away from me.

Trenton's light-brown eyes sparkle in amusement. "We are. You asked if he is alright." He lifts his hand and drags his fingertips over my cheek. "Hayes is pretty good at catching certain types of lies."

He doesn't say it in a demeaning way — doesn't act as though my cheek is the only lie Hayes has picked up on. He just simply states a fact about his best friend, all the while his fingertips promise protection and gentleness.

I have been backed into an uncomfortable corner and am so out of my element that I don't know how to respond. With a hard swallow, I lift my chin and gently press that side of my face into his palm. "What do you want me to say, Trenton?" I ask on a whisper.

"Give me a name. Car make and model. Something."

"No." I steal a quick, hopefully unnoticed, glance over his shoulder to check on the progress of Jude and Porter getting the hell out of here. Porter is closing the hood and Jude is climbing back into the driver's seat. When my attention returns, Trenton's gaze is narrowed on mine.

I close my eyes to escape the scrutiny. "This… whatever this is between you, Hayes, and me… I like it. This" — I press my bruised cheek against his palm, squeezing my eyes shut tighter when it smarts — "needs to stay separate."

His thumb brushes against my jaw. I take the opportunity to inch closer to him. So close, I can hear his breathing over the din of engines and enthusiasts.

When I do open my eyes, his gaze pierces mine before dropping to my mouth, the slight tick of a smile creeping up on his. When I dart a quick glance over his shoulder again, Jude and Porter are gone.

"So, you like this thing between the three of us, hm?" he asks, moving his thumb to trace my bottom lip. Thankful that Trenton knows when to drop a topic and send a boost of excitement to otherwise uncomfortable situations, my raised chin drops and shoulders loosen.

The problem is, his touch and the confident speech is electrifying and so easily veers me off track. As much as I like this budding…

Friendship?

No, friends don't try to collect information for a takeover.

Acquaintance?

I don't know… that doesn't seem quite fitting either.

Anyway, as much as I like this connection with them, it can't turn into anything more than what it already is. Anything more than the occasional cruise down The Strip or a quick lay.

"Yeah… having friends in a new area is nice." The word "friends" leaves my tongue heavy and thick.

The confidence lighting up Trenton's face dims for a blink, but he bounces back quickly. "Swear this will be the last I beat around the bush tonight about the topic that is supposed to 'stay separate.'" I raise a brow and he continues. "Our offer for a place to escape to remains. That's what friends are for, after all… right?"

Ugh… if he would just stop being so damn nice, maybe this would be easier. I stick with a simple, curt nod. He doesn't skip a beat, though, moving right along. "Now, I promised you a night out. You still up for that?"

"This meetup isn't what you had in mind?"

"Mm, part of it. But, not quite. Crow, Hayes, and I usually dip out on these before everyone else does unless there's a reason for us to stick around. I was hoping to take you with us this time."

"Crow? Are you sure he is going to be okay with that?"

"Nope. But I have an idea… if you're up for helping me give him a hard time? The three of us are always fucking with each other, and it's his turn to get a surprise. That little tête-à-tête between the two of you gave me a good idea."

Honestly, it sounds fun. Plus, if I can somehow get closer to Crow, all the better. "Count me in," I answer with a combo bite to my bottom lip and smile.

Trenton groans. "If we're keeping this as a 'just friends' thing, you're going to have to stop doing shit like that." Fire lights in his eyes. "You make me stupid enough as it is just by" — he waves his hands at me — "being."

Yeah, hot stuff, apparently the feeling is mutual since that is literally what he makes me. Stupid. Mute. Unable to do something so seemingly simple like ask about a street racing club.

To prove the point, a silly grin bunches up my cheeks. "So… this plan to mess with Crow. What can I do to help?"

"First, do me a favor and park behind the restaurant? If you're okay with leaving it here for a few hours?"

"Yeah, not a problem. Now?"

"Yep, now is good."

184

After handing Trenton my phone to hold, I walk the short distance to where I had temporarily parked, sling my leg over the seat, pop the kickstand, and start her up, not bothering to put on the helmet. As usual, several eyes turn toward me.

Trenton meets me around back. As soon as I'm off the bike and have removed my clutch purse from the storage compartment, he hands my phone back, and I pocket it with my keyless remote. "Why aren't your cars up front with the rest?" I ask, having noticed right away that the Monte, Bimmer, and Supra are all back here. He slips his hand around my shoulders and guides me over to Crow's car.

"Eh, they all know what we drive. And… none of us care to share what's beneath the hood. Not at a meetup like this."

Oooh… tell me more…

Trenton looks over his shoulder toward the side of the building, to check for anyone approaching, I presume. He digs out a set of keys. The Supra honks and its lights flash when Trenton pushes a button on the fob. The click of a lock disengaging echoes through the night.

The first night that I had witnessed Crow and Trenton interact, I could tell right away they were on good terms. Plus, I can't imagine it being easy for Trenton to get ahold of Crow's keys if they were anything but, so I choose to trust whatever is going on.

185

Until Trenton opens the passenger door, steps back, and gestures for me to get in.

My mouth drops open as I gasp and take a few steps back, holding out a hand. "Wait. You… want me to get inside without his permission?"

Trenton's affable grin spreads. "Hell yes I do."

My heartbeat triples as my gaze trails from nose to bumper.

Ohh, he is going to be pissed.

Do I want to be the recipient of his anger?

What type of anger is it?

As though Trenton can read exactly what's going through my mind, he drops his hand. "No… he'll be surprised, but he… he won't take it out on you. All you need to do is tell him I put you up to it. He'll know who to place the blame on right away. Swear." With the swear he draws a cross over his heart with his thumb.

CHAPTER TWENTY-EIGHT

Not wanting to back out of the challenge I already committed to, I step forward, eating up the distance I had lost while retreating. I sit on the edge of the black leather, toe off my shoes, and adjust in the seat. Trenton watches, fascinated. As soon as I am situated, he closes me inside. I peer into the side mirror through the dark-tinted window as he walks back to the front of the restaurant.

The hammering in my chest hasn't ceased since he told me of this plan, and now that I am sitting here inside Crow's car it only worsens. I place my clutch and shoes on the floorboard, fold my hands in my lap like a child who has been told not to touch anything, and scan what I can see of the interior in the mix of pure night and swarthy design.

My gaze catches on a solid red button, a stark difference amid all the black, and the reminder of what I am supposed to be doing slams into me yet again. My heart rate kicks up another notch, and I unclasp my hands.

I trace the crimson circle with my finger, take a deep breath, then turn around seeking out its purpose.

Just as I suspected, tanks of nitrous are mounted in the trunk within easy reach to be turned on with the flick of a wrist.

I've seen a fair share of gearheads attempt to hide their tanks. Seems Crow has no trouble with honesty where the interior setup of this mod is concerned.

My cellphone burns a hole in my pocket; the weight of needing to contact Jude and Porter and give them the closest thing to an answer I have gotten singes its way through my clothing.

Wanting to do Jude proud, despite wishing for this to be over with already, I let it be. There is still more information to dig up. Still more details and specifics. Still more puzzle pieces to flip and fit. Because even though more and more signs point to the fact that these guys equip their cars to race, that doesn't mean they are the club owners or have anything to do with the specific underground racing club we're looking for.

The pop of a door handle lifting and snapping back has me spinning around in the seat and pressing my back hard into its curve, knees shaking. The pulse that had started to dull races all over again.

Crow enters, every inky inch of him blending into the interior from his crow-colored hair to his clothing and tattoos. With his left foot still on the ground outside the car door and his right hand pinching the key between thumb and pointer, he jolts, head slinging toward me and keys dropping to the floorboard.

"Sonuvabitch," he grumbles, bending down to locate his keys.

Wringing my hands, the corner of my bottom lip slips between my teeth.

Once his keys are collected, he leans back into the seat, still not committed to being inside his car with a stranger by bringing in the foot that remains outside.

He slips the key into the ignition but doesn't turn it. His hand — numbers tattooed atop each knuckle — lifts, and he drags his palm over his mouth before gripping the wheel. A sleeve tattoo bulges on account of the flexing of his bicep from the movement. "Why the fuck are you in my car?" Black venom spews from his perfectly shaped lips… accentuated by that middle lip ring on the bottom.

Goddammit he is hella sexy.

"Favor for a friend."

His upper teeth gleam in contrast to the shadowy surroundings as he drags them over the piercing. He curses Trenton under his breath, slinging a scathing leer out the driver's side window.

I bend down and pick up my shoes and clutch with one hand while hooking my finger into the door handle with the other.

Movement draws my gaze over my left shoulder for one last glimpse as I start to open the door. His bright silvery eyes — so opposite everything else about him — sweep from my belongings to my bare toes that now curve over the side sill and back up to my face.

"Close the door," he states. Since I have little to no control of myself around guys like him, I inch my toes back inside and gently obey the command. "I'll never fucking hear the end of it if you get out. That's what Trenton is expecting, so that's exactly what he's not going to get."

My attention moves past his shoulder. Both Hayes and Trenton's cars are on, headlights shining into the copse of trees that separates the properties in front of us. Waiting.

When my gaze returns to Crow, his tongue is looping around that damn lip ring, mouth half-cocked in a smirk.

My heart, stomach, and thighs clench.

"This is great. Do you know just how damn badly Trenton wants you to ride with him tonight?"

Tongue heavy, throat tight, I can do nothing more than stare out the window.

Crow drops his voice to a whisper, head tilted down slightly. "He is fucking gutted over you. Getting you in his car — and bed — again is all he can think about."

Emblazoned with a hit of counterfeit confidence, I return my attention to him. "Same thing has been on my mind," I share. It isn't a total lie. Okay, it isn't a lie at all. "One of the best one-night stands I've ever had," I share unabashedly.

"Yeah? Well neither of you are getting what you want tonight." His lips curve in a full-blown, dangerous gleam. "Looks like you're stuck with me. Trenton is about to learn a damn lesson."

Without further ado, he turns the engine and puts her in reverse before even giving me a say. Not that I would choose the alternative. Trenton is fun, but after seeing Crow's setup, I have a feeling he is where the answers are. Maybe this will all come to a head tonight.

He eases us out of the parking lot while I click the seat belt into place. I dig my hair clip out of my pocket, preparing for the launch control guys with cars like these so often like to perform. Especially on an unsuspecting passenger.

With twin turbos and a fucking nitrous system, I would be more surprised if he *didn't* show off a little.

By the time he has straightened on the road, my hair is up, the clip tightly secured.

From what I understand about the tourist off-season in areas like these, roads are a racer's dream at this time of night. We approach the first red light, a nice empty stretch spanning ahead of us. My eyes flick to the side mirror and find Hayes's passenger-side light shining.

The click of a flipped switch coaxes my focus back to Crow just as he drops his hand from the steering wheel and his finger depresses a small button near the gearshift. Despite itching to grab the door grip handle with one hand and the console with the other, I place each hand on my thighs loosely.

Here we go.

My gaze falls to his lap, and I watch as his actions mirror my predictions: both hands fist the steering wheel, his left thigh bunches under his jeans, and his right thigh soon mimics the motion.

My eyes return to his face, and his dart sideways toward me, tongue swiping across his lower lip, pausing only briefly on the ring in the center. For a flash, all I can think about is how badly I want those hands… and that tongue… on me.

Belt on, hair up, body loose, I listen and feel as he slowly presses the accelerator and the engine revs, creating a steady hum beneath us.

There is one main reason why car guys pull out fast from a dead stop with a female passenger in their car — to get a reaction out of them.

Unfortunately for Crow, I am not the type of girl who squeals and tenses from speed.

The light turns green, the engine rasps, and gravity forces my body to melt into the seat from the force until he switches gears and I jerk forward, nearly face planting into his dash. The seat belt does its job, preventing me from doing so.

Pretty sure the mass I just swallowed was my entire heart. It doesn't matter if you are raised in the scene. If you've been in the passenger seat of more fast vehicles than you can count on your fingers and toes. It doesn't matter how many launch controls you experience, your blood turns into pure adrenaline and your heart will go from zero to sixty in two seconds right along with the car.

I let a pent-up breath out slowly through my nose, moderating the threat of my chest rising and falling too hard as he slows down to a more manageable speed. Once smoothed out, I spot the swivel of his head in my peripheral and turn mine toward him. A single brow is raised on his handsome face.

Instead of giving him a verbal response or a smirk, I simply remove the clip from my hair and let the dark strands cascade over my shoulders. As much as I like my hair down, I didn't particularly want to eat it — or need to finger out knots — on account of it fanning everywhere from the recoil.

A quiet chuckle meets my ear as his focus returns to the road.

For the rest of the drive, I try extra hard to make the hum and wetness between my legs lessen.

CHAPTER TWENTY-NINE

My lungs ache to pull in a deep, recovery breath, but I manage to control my body's natural urge to not drown in the overproduction of adrenaline. To aid in my efforts, I let my senses drift to the way the Supra feels on the road compared to the Monte and Bimmer. The Supra is lighter, smoother, and not nearly as vocal as the Monte Carlo. The Bimmer and Supra show more similarities. But this is still a bit more... spirited... than the Bimmer. More aggressive, in a way.

The incessant rush pumping through my veins and that damn buzz connecting Crow and me, despite both our efforts to pretend it's not there, gift me the brazenness I've been lacking. With little forethought, I'm asking the question I had worked so hard to not just straight out ask. But the *ren* of the engine and *wom* of tires over asphalt creates an atmosphere that makes the question just seem right and appropriate: "Do you run it?"

Crow's hand tightens over the shift knob as he switches gear. The car tugs. "Race? No."

Receiving the opposite answer from what I'd expected blanches my blood, leeching every bit of remaining adrenaline and draining it away.

A sense of foreboding failure seeps into my veins instead. It takes all of my willpower to not slam my palms on the dashboard in frustration.

Breathing more intensely now than I was just moments ago, I close my eyes and drop my head back against the headrest. "But you have nitrous," I mutter, still somewhat disbelieving.

"Yeah? I have a cock, too. Doesn't mean I use it every time I take my pants off."

My eyes flare open and I jerk my attention toward him. "When do you use it then, exactly?" I ask.

"My cock or my nitrous?"

Funny thing is, I'm not entirely sure which I'm more curious about at this point. When I pin him with an unamused stare, he flashes those top teeth again, catching his piercing behind them.

"Special occasions, and generally when no one else is involved." Crow doesn't elaborate to which of the two he is referring.

I examine the red button. Inspection moving to his lap, my mind has absolutely no trouble visualizing his tattooed knuckles gripping his stick and working it like a pro.

Both types.

When my perusal finally reaches his face again, he's donning the smuggest of expressions. "I think I'm starting to understand why Trenton is so infatuated with you."

When I don't press, because I have somehow forgotten how to organize thoughts into appropriate conversation, he continues. "You're fucking hungry. Keep looking at me like that, and cruising in my car isn't the only thing we'll be doing together tonight." To further his point, he boldly drops his hand to his lap and adjusts himself.

"Don't rev next to me unless you intend on showing me what you've got." My fingers twitch to jerk up and cover my mouth.

Crow's eyes darken to a steely chrome, jaw moving over clenched teeth. Both of us unsure which topic our back and forth is referring to mostly. Whichever it was, Crow is done. The tug of war over.

At some point during our conversation, we'd traveled the distance from beach to bay side. I had tried to ignore the way my heart thudded at the sight of shrimp boats and the scent of marine fuel. Focus riveting to the passenger mirror as a distraction, I watch as two sets of headlights follow us into the marina. Much smaller in size than the ports I had grown accustomed to, but still all too familiar.

The scene pulls me under no matter how hard I try to ignore the threat of flashbacks. Grasping for an out, my eyes search the area, looking for all the differences, for any and everything that would replace the last memory in my mind of a docking area. Of betrayal and murder.

Crow swings into the open parking area, lining the nose of his car up with the railing that overlooks the bay, and suddenly I am back in Cali on a port, revisiting the night my dad was brutally murdered right in front of me.

My entire body freezes, just as it had that night. Frozen in terror as I watch the scene replay in my mind. A gust of fish and fuel-infused air blows across my face. A warm, firm grip, wraps around my upper arms. "Remi!" the panicked masculine voice whisper-yells. "We need to get you out of here. Come on."

Porter's voice flows through the memory while the nearby voice nearly replicates the same words from that horrible night. Déjà vu in the worst way.

"Fuck. What the hell did you say to her, Burke?!" Trenton chastises. The new, unfamiliar name seems to be what tugs me back to the present.

"Remi..." This comes from Hayes. I blink a few times until his midnight-blue eyes come into a wet and blurry view. As soon as he recognizes that I am no longer mentally somewhere else, he adjusts his glasses on the bridge of his nose and lets out a breath of relief. "Let's get you out of the car, okay? Walk around a little so you can get some air. Sports cars like his can be tight and constricting for people not used to them."

My head shakes of its own accord. If anything, I feel safer from the memory inside the car, not walking around and having little things here and there act as horrific reminders.

"No?" Hayes pops the glovebox, takes out a napkin, and dabs at the wetness on my face.

With every pat, I calm down a little. Aside from the occasional nightmare, a single flashback of that night had not consumed me. I'd been able to lock the memory deep inside, only for it to peek through when my subconscious insisted. Even then, I would jolt myself from sleep before it got out of hand.

The small amount of counseling Jude insisted we get before moving taught me that even despite putting up the strongest mental shutters and fortifications, our minds can regress, causing locked-away memories to resurface.

Hayes doesn't press while I work through things in my mind — while I overcome the unwelcome flashback and try to get past it. "I just need a couple minutes."

"Panic attacks... flashbacks... do they happen to you often?" Hayes asks.

Catching sight of Trenton and Crow over his shoulder, who are engaged in a serious conversation that consists of flailing arms and tensing muscles, I shake my head. "Crow didn't do anything. It had nothing to do with him. It... it just sorta happened."

Hayes follows my sightline before returning his attention to me. "Okay, I'll let Trenton know Crow is allowed to live to see another day."

A watery chuckle leaves me. "I'll handle it. Sorry about this... talking to them myself is the least I can do for ruining all the fun."

Hayes's eyebrows pinch together. "You sure?"

"Yeah." I slip on my shoes and angle my body to get out of the car. Hayes stands and holds his hand out. My gaze drops to his fingers and back up to his glasses-rimmed eyes again. I wrap my hand into his, and he gives me a warm smile as he helps me out of the car. Then, he drops his hand and shoves both into his pockets as we walk side by side over to Crow and Trenton.

Both men shut up, pressing their lips together as soon as I approach. Suddenly shy and embarrassed, I speak toward the concrete ground. "Sorry. Crow didn't do anything. Something... triggered a panic attack when we drove up. Nothing to do with driving or riding."

Movement has my gaze lifting back to the guys. Crow crosses his arms over his chest and cocks an eyebrow at Trenton. Trenton deflates a little. "I thought maybe that launch control stunt he pulled scared you or something."

A laugh bursts out of me. "Takes more than a little launch control to scare me."

"A… a little launch control? His car is a damn rocket! That shit scares me," Trenton gasps.

Hayes cracks a grin. "I have a feeling Remi knows even more about vehicles than she lets on."

Blocking out all the secrets each wave lapping against the docking slips whispers, I cross my arms and state: "I know a thing or two." Taking the opportunity to tell them some, without revealing all, and to use their friendship as somewhat of a therapy outlet, I let one of the more pleasant memories of my father tumble from my lips, hoping it'll help loosen the vice on my heart. "My dad was a single parent. He ate, slept, and breathed vehicles. Dinner conversation with my brother and him often revolved around engine types and body styles. I may have always acted bored, but I listened and absorbed every bit. Anyway, that panic attack… or whatever it was… that's the first time it has happened. I am truly sorry. And embarrassed as hell."

Last thing any of these guys want is a high-maintenance girl. They spend enough time on car maintenance as it stands.

The three of them share a look. Crow drops his arms from his chest, Hayes shrugs, and Trenton blinks once before giving me a nod of acknowledgement. "Things like that happen. We just don't want to make you uncomfortable."

"Oh, no… I feel very comfortable around you." The confession is out of my mouth spontaneously, proving just how visceral the statement is.

However, having learned that Crow does not race, my strongest lead has come to an abrupt stop at a dead end.

Part of me feels liberated at that revelation. The part that wants to see where this uncanny physical and emotional connection goes with them — minus the deception that brought us together.

The other part of me wants to leave, hop on my bike, and peruse the forums again so I can steer back onto the right course.

Right now, I am stuck here unless I ask one of them to take me back. But I had promised Trenton he could take me out, and here we are. There's no harm in finishing up this route with a bit of fun before redirecting.

And maybe, just maybe, I can keep them as friends.

Or something more.

CHAPTER THIRTY

A strange silence figure eights around the four of us for a few heartbeats too long before Crow pipes in. "Did you load the cooler back up?"

Trenton leads the way toward his car, pops the trunk, peers over his shoulder, and states, "We have sodas, waters, and beers. Pick your poison."

"Guess since I'm not driving, I'll take a beer," I answer. Trenton pulls out a bottle and tosses it to Hayes. Hayes seems to have expected this and catches it easy. Placing the bottle cap flush against his forearm, he twists his arm and the top pops off. When he holds the beer out, I accept it, taking a step forward as I ogle his forearms. Unashamedly curious, I place my hand on his arm and push up his three-quarter-length sleeve, seeking hidden muscles.

Crow snorts and says, "In case anyone is wondering what it is he does in his bedroom all the time, now you know."

My fingers trail over the dips of his forearms and up under the somewhat folded cuff of his shirt, wrapping around the bicep that is, indeed, bigger than I had anticipated.

"Impressive." I give him a playful wink and squeeze.

Hayes turns beet red, and Crow mumbles "Unbelievable."

Rubbing the back of his neck with the arm not presently being fondled by me, he pins Crow with an unamused glare. "Um… you don't need big forearm muscles to open a beer bottle. In fact… it's the fat there that provides the support."

I look down at my own arm, and a quiet laugh comes from Hayes. He leans forward and whispers in my ear, "Want me to teach you? Crow will be pissed."

My lips quirk upward and I nod. With his face so close to mine, my temple grazes the slight stubble on his cheek.

Their love of messing with each other rubs off on me for some reason. Especially when it comes to Crow. He just seems fun to mess with.

Hayes straightens. "Hook me up with a couple more," he yells over my shoulder, sidestepping around me.

Trenton grabs two more and tosses them our direction. Hayes catches the first one, wedges it between his thighs and catches the second before removing the first and jerking his head to the side, gesturing for me to follow.

He leads me to the end of the concrete dock, dips under the railing and sits down, legs dangling over the edge. I follow suit. The concrete scuffs the underside of my thighs. Looking down into the dark, undulating water gives me a bit of vertigo, so I take a brief moment to squeeze my eyes shut and inhale the salty air.

When I open my eyes, Hayes is staring out at the twinkling lights of barges and other large-scale ships in the far distance. "Do they dock here?" I ask.

"The big ones here at the marina? Nah. The PC port just opened a new terminal, so we're starting to see a lot more traffic."

That explains a whole heck of a lot. When Jude had said we'd be moving over here, I could swear I remembered Dad mentioning that the best ports were in Jax or Pensacola. Both roughly two to three hours from where we're living now. It didn't make sense to me why Jude would want to set up shop so far away from the port if he was intending on carrying on some of the Lance Industries business in this area.

Not that we need to be right on a port, but it sure makes certain types of dealings easier.

"You know a lot about water vessels, too?" Hayes asks, picking up one of the unopened beers he'd placed between us.

"Oh... um... it's a vehicle, isn't it?" A playful smile teases at my lips as I take the first sip of my beer.

"Yeah, it is." He picks at the damp label on the bottle.

"I'm kidding, kinda. I know a little about certain boats, but not as much as I do about street vehicles."

He holds up the unopened beer, tilting it in my direction. I take another quick drink from mine and place it down on my opposite side before accepting the unopened one.

"The biggest mistakes most people make when trying to open a bottle with their forearm is turning the bottle instead of the arm, twisting the wrong way, or not pushing hard enough because they're afraid it'll hurt. But, if you do it right, the top should pop right off, pain free."

I press the top of the cap against my forearm where I had seen him place it earlier and look up at him for approval.

Instead of picking up the second bottle, his fingers curve around the ledge on either side of his thighs, and he leans forward slightly, nearly giving me a heart attack. "Hayes, if you fall in, I can't save you."

He laughs and leans back, resting his upper back against the railing. "Well in that case, guess I should be careful. Because I sure as hell wouldn't want Trenton or Crow saving me."

I press my lips together to hold back the giddy grin trying to reveal itself. Pretty sure that's the most flirty thing he has said to me outright. It's cute. And sweet. And I kinda want to hear more.

I hold my arm up, top of the bottle pressed into my flesh, and elevate an eyebrow in silent inquiry.

Hayes inclines his head in acceptance. "Hold tight and firm with your right hand, do all the twisting with your left arm." The smile I had been trying to hide morphs into a giggle at his choice of words for the instructions.

My giggling has a contagious effect on him and he chuckles, too. "We're talking about a beer bottle, Remi. Get your mind out of the gutter."

"Sorry." One more giggle burbles out of me before I slam my mouth shut, clear my throat, and put on my most serious face.

"Twist inward, toward your chest. Most importantly, though, press harder than you think you might need to. It's better to press too hard than not hard enough. You'll tear your arm up if you don't do it hard enough."

I bob my head resolutely, the action serving two purposes. One, to let him know I understand. And two, to give myself a boost of confidence.

Hayes sits up straight again so he can watch more closely. I don't waste any time thinking about how it might not work. If I think too hard about it, my chances of failing increase exponentially.

Pressing the cap as deep into my flesh as possible, almost to the point I am convinced it'll leave a bruise, I twist my arm toward my chest. I can't hear the release of pressure over the slapping of waves against the concrete wall, but the cap loosens under my arm. I hold it up proudly, and the cap falls into the bay.

Hayes leans against the railing again beaming proudly. "Got it on the first try. Good job."

His palm ghosts across my upper thighs as he reaches to wrap his fingers over the cool glass. The bottle exchanges hands as our eyes lock, and I reach back to pick up my own beer again. Tilting the bottle toward him, I offer cheers. He accepts, clinking his glass against mine before taking a sip. "Ready to show Crow up?" he asks, licking the first taste of beer off his bottom lip.

"Yeah. Happily," I respond — a bit dreamily if I'm being fully honest. The connection finally breaks when he has to pick up the second unopened beer, hold the necks of both bottles between curved fingers of one hand, and use his opposite hand to turn around and duck back under the railing.

Watching him use only one hand as support on the relatively narrow ledge between the deep water and metal rails, gives me heart palpitations. Nonetheless, he manages just fine, having apparently done it a time… or twenty.

Not feeling nearly as adept, I opt to hand him my beer before attempting the feat myself. As soon as my body is angled toward the railing, vertigo hits again.

I quickly grab the railing and hoist myself up so I can grip it with both hands. Once the water is at my back and I feel more stable, I sling my leg between the bars and crouch through.

CHAPTER THIRTY-ONE

"If you really want to show off," Hayes explains, handing me the closed beer, "remove your arm from the top slowly so the cap stays balanced. When you hold the bottle up, flick the cap off with your wrist or finger. Adds a bit of flare."

"How is it that you know so much about this, but you don't drink often. Kinda like how Crow has nitrous but doesn't race?" I hadn't meant to add the part about Crow, but it just sorta came out. Hayes comes to a halt. "He told you that?"

I stop a couple paces in front of him before doubling back. "Yeah. Well, not about the nitrous; that part I saw for myself. But, when I asked if he races, he said no." Lifting a shoulder, I elaborate: "Guess it just seemed strange that he would have that sort of setup, but not race with it. Was he lying?"

Hayes starts walking again, leading me toward Trenton and Crow who are setting up some discarded shipping crates in the very center of the desolate parking lot. "No… he told the truth. I'm just surprised he answered the question at all."

Remembering I'd asked Hayes a similar question during our first ride together, I want to say *"What, and avoid it Like you did?"* but I choose to refrain from ruining the moment with unnecessary scrutiny.

Even despite the apparently stalled search, my intuition is screaming otherwise. There are too many flags. Too many coincidences.

Feeling confident and safe with Hayes, I cast yet another line: "With his nitrous, Trenton having aftermarket gauges, and your harness seat belts, I guess I just began to assume…"

Hayes stops short of our destination again. This time he turns to me, both our beers skillfully hooked with the fingers of one hand and dangling between us. He adjusts his glasses with the other hand. "If you hadn't been inside our vehicles, would you have picked up the same impression?"

Thinking about it for a minute, I determine that aside from the forum, their cars are exactly why I chose to continue perusing the trail. "Maybe a little. Nothing more than a bit of curiosity, I suppose. The sticky tires on Crow's car were really the only thing between the three of your vehicles that made me wonder before seeing the inside. But, then again, he drives a Supra… so performance tires aren't all that unusual."

Hayes looks up at me from a slightly downward tilted head, his eyes reaching over the frame of his glasses. He looks as though there's something else he wants to say, but he simply nods and moves one of the beers from his looped fingers so that he is holding one in each hand.

When we continue walking, I assume the conversation is over, but he asks one final question, pulling off so easily what I keep floundering to do: "Do you race?"

My heart and stomach do a triple jump in sync. "I have. I will. But not often. I like speed and am a bit of an adrenaline junkie. That's why I stick with riding a motorcycle. I love how strapping on my helmet and opening the throttle are equal parts terrifying and thrilling. Every time. The feeling never gets old. But... organized racing? No. Never been part of that scene."

It feels good being able to answer honestly for once, without giving away incriminating evidence to my original intentions. Feeling even bolder now, I once again ask the same question of him. "How about you?"

His fingers twitch against the bottles. "Mm... I've been known to roll and dig a little."

"Trenton?" I ask quietly, both hope and trepidation rising inside. "All go and no show?"

Hayes choke-laughs. "Does he know you realize his car is a sleeper?"

"Yeah, it's one of the first things we talked about when I rode with him."

Hayes shakes his head in disbelief. "No wonder he proposed marriage." He clears his throat and drops his voice to a whisper. "Don't tell him I told you this, but he joked about taking you as a wife the night he first saw you. Before all the… moaning and screaming and stuff."

I laugh… loud enough that both Trenton and Crow snap to attention. Their focus leaves the crates for a second before returning to stack on a fourth. Since I have a free hand and Hayes doesn't, I slap his arm. "So you did hear us!"

"Us?" he says, amused. "No… I heard *you*. Rattling just like that dry clutch on your Duc."

I narrow an unamused glare at him, and he chuckles. His face turns bright red under the lot lights, and he lets out a slow breath. "It was hot."

A sudden and unexpected warm breeze swirls around us. An image of Hayes enjoying himself while Trenton made me cry out in pleasure over and over again plays in my mind. The muscles he keeps hidden tensing with each stroke—

Hayes watches the tips of his shoes with every forward step. But he seems to feel my attention on him, and his gaze lifts in my direction, tongue dragging across his bottom lip.

That spot between my spine and below my belly button tightens. He doesn't have to verbalize what he did when hearing my sex noises through the wall in his bedroom; the truth is written in the heaviness of his eyelids, damp lips, and the new bulge in his pants.

Crow was right… I am hungry. There has never been an issue with my libido. But these guys seem to somehow kick an already healthy and curious drive into a higher gear.

Maybe I like car guys more than I thought I did.

Maybe I've been lying to myself all these years.

Or…

Maybe it is just these particular car guys…

CHAPTER THIRTY-TWO

"**S**how time," Hayes whispers out of the corner of his mouth.

"Crow…" I draw out his name, instantly earning his attention. He raises a black eyebrow in response. "I brought you a beer."

Crow gives Hayes and Trenton shifty eyes, definitely untrusting of the scenario. Trenton joins in, tilting his head at Hayes in silent inquiry. Hayes doesn't humor either of them. Instead, he takes a long pull from his own beer, still keeping mine held loosely at his side.

I wiggle the unopened beer in display before pushing it against my forearm and quickly, but efficiently, twisting… keeping the loose cap balanced while I pull the bottle away. I hadn't realized until Crow crosses his arms and gives me a smug grin that by doing that, it has given him the impression my attempt didn't work. So, Crow gets a brief moment of smugness, darting an unamused glance at Hayes, who he has now determined put me up to this task.

When his attention returns to me, though, I…

Well, I don't know why I decide to opt out of the suggested wrist or finger flip. Instead, I loop my tongue around the loose cap until the tip slips under the ragged metal and the cap lifts off. Then, I wrap my lips around the entire cap and pull it off that way.

The smug grin disappears from Crow's face, replaced by the toying of his labret piercing. With a smug grin of my own, I step close to him and press the now-opened beer against his chest. Eyes on that damn piercing, I carefully remove the cap from my mouth, making sure to clean any lingering saliva with my tongue and lips as I pull it free.

That burning, fiery tension between us ignites. The one I know without a doubt he feels too. Crow wraps his fingers around mine, and slowly removes the beer from my grip, bringing it up to his mouth, eyes on me all the while.

Jesus, that mouth.

And those eyes.

"Thanks," he says after bringing the bottle down.

"Anytime," I breathlessly respond.

He rubs his free hand across his mouth, dragging it down to cup his chin ever so briefly before dropping his hand.

A mutter of unintelligible words comes from our right, pulling my focus away from the walking, living, breathing, danger over to Trenton. "Mm… damn you are something else." He throws his head back and groans. So wrapped up in Crow for a moment, I had forgotten that the man I slept with who has become increasingly intrigued by me — and me with him if I allow myself the honesty of such a novelty — is right beside us, watching my flirting firsthand. The flirting that in this instance was not with him, but with, yet again, another one of his friends. However... he doesn't seem bothered by it.

Who am I kidding? That was far, far beyond just flirting.

I dare a step backward. Not to retreat or escape from the fire incinerating our souls, but to prevent myself from stoking the flame too much more.

Crow's hand darts out and captures my wrist. He yanks me forward — and my body responds in the worst way: enjoying it.

"Three strikes, and you're out," he threatens.

The first strike being whatever the hell that back and forth was in the car?

This being the second?

What happens after the third one?

"Crow..." one of the other guys warns. So enraptured by this man, my mind can't seem to pick up who gave the warning.

"No... it's okay," I breathe out. Our faces are so close now that my warm, beery breath bounces right back at me. "I'm all too familiar with guys like him. All bark and no bite."

Ohh... is that strike three?

Crow lets out a low, menacing chuckle, letting me go. He shakes the mouth of his beer at me as I step back. "You… are fucking trouble."

"Funny" — I reach for my beer from Hayes and take a demure sip — "I keep thinking the exact same thing about you."

And together?

We'd paint the town.

The two of us stand staring at each other for an indiscernible amount of time. Eventually, Trenton claps his hands together and whoops, jolting us out of the stare down.

Our heads turn toward Trenton at the same time.

Trenton's expression lights up. "Ready?"

Crow grins, and his eyes sparkle mischievously.

I suddenly remember why car guys are typically a pain in the ass: they're thrill seekers, hardwired to do something audacious and crazy.

Trenton takes my free hand and drags me over to the stacked crates. He climbs on top first, takes my beer, places it down, then holds both hands out.

I grip them and scale the stack until he launches me up the rest of the way, ending the motion with a playful slap to the ass. I dart an equally playful glance over my shoulder at him as I bend over, keeping my knees straight and tight as I dramatically pick my beer back up.

"Mmmm," Trenton groans, biting down on his bottom lip and shaking his head. He cups a hand over his mouth and yells toward Crow and Hayes, "Someone get me a damn drink!"

Both guys head toward the cars. Crow is the one who caters to Trenton this time, grabbing one out of the cooler. Meanwhile, Hayes hops into his car.

Crow jogs back toward the crates, and when he's close enough, he chucks a bottle at Trenton. Unlike Hayes, Trenton fumbles to catch it.

"Fuck you!" he yells as Crow runs back toward his car. When Crow is no longer in sight, Trenton eyes the water bottle with distaste.

The look of disappointment draws a laugh out of me. "Want to swap?" I ask. "Mine is getting a little warm, but I'm happy to share."

"Nah. I'm not sure how much more you three are going to drink. But considering Hayes usually doesn't partake, looks like I might be driving all four of us back tonight."

"Hayes and Crow would leave their vehicles here overnight?"

"Yeah. Everyone in roughly a three county radius recognizes their vehicles. No one is going to do anything. Plus" — he points somewhere in the distance and I follow the direction — "cameras."

Again, my stomach twists, wrapped in past memories. "Do all marinas have security systems?"

More so, was Dad's death recorded?

"Yes. Always. Whether or not it matters depends on money and influence."

Does that mean Hayes and Crow have money and influence?

Crow's verbal reprimand about me coming from money flashes in my thoughts. He wasn't wrong. But someone owning a Duc is hardly enough proof that a person comes from money.

Besides, on account of recent happenings, the money dynamic of my life has changed significantly.

CHAPTER THIRTY-THREE

"**S**o, what are we doing?" I ask, plopping onto my butt on the edge of the crates. Unlike being on the edge of the water, this doesn't give me vertigo, thank goodness.

"Well, for starters, you're going to stand back up," Trenton explains.

"Oh…" I reach behind me for support and push back up to standing. "Okay, Sir."

Trenton waggles his brows at me and reaches behind his head, whipping his shirt off in one, smooth motion. My eyes instantly go googly-eyed and dazed. Damn this man's body.

Him and Hayes must be eating the same chicken.

Or drinking the same water.

Or… probably hitting the same gym.

Yeah… that.

He holds his shirt out to me. With a raised brow, I take it. At the same time, Hayes and Crow's vehicles roar to life. The two immediately roll into reverse. Crow straightens and backs up again so he is positioned facing the crates, rear bumper nearly touching the marina railing, nose pointed at the right side of our setup.

Hayes loops around the lot until he is positioned toward the crates on the opposite right side. Their headlights create stage lighting where Trenton and I stand about five feet from the ground.

"Know anything about signaling?" Trenton asks.

My attention seesaws from Hayes and Crow back to him. "Yeah…"

"Show us what you've got then," he says with a wink and grin.

Usually when signaling, we stand on the dividing line in front of the two racers, point at each and wait for a nod, then raise our arms — and the flag, if applicable — and drop them.

But this time, the "racers" are facing each other, and there is no road ahead nor behind them. The only thing that keeps me from drilling Trenton about what the hell they're going to do is just how cringey most women are about these things — squealing and frightened. And I'm not that type of woman.

Scanning the scene, I decide on facing sideways, neither toward Hayes nor Crow. I place my beer down and stuff an edge of Trenton's shirt into the front of my shorts.

Once I'm in position, Trenton faces me on the opposite edge of the crates, grins, and cups his hands to project his voice.

I continue to study the scene as both racers lean out of their windows, waiting for cues from Trenton and me. Trenton turns his hand-style megaphone toward Crow and says, "To our right…"

I point at the black Supra to my right — Trenton's left — and Trenton continues, "we have Crow, driving a…"

He holds a fake microphone to my mouth. Eyes wide and one thick swallow later, I announce, "Six-cylinder, mid-90s Supra with twin turbos."

Crow revs and holds up a hand, finger raised.

Trenton nods, impressed, curving his mouth down in an expression that reminds me of something like what an Italian might do. "To our left, we have…"

Again, he provides me with a fake microphone. "Hayes, representing an E30?" — I drop my voice, grimacing, and whisper to Trenton, "I think his is completely custom… a swap?"

"Fuck… I think I just busted a load in my shorts." A laugh bursts out of me. Trenton adjusts himself and whispers even lower, "Supra motor; 2JZ engine; T56 American transmission."

Well, holy shit.

With my own impressed nod and Italian-like gesture, I point toward Hayes and repeat the details, hopefully loud enough that the racers can hear.

Hayes revs and pats the outside of his door.

Trenton removes the invisible microphone, our eyes meet, I pluck his shirt from between my shorts, lift the material up high, and drop both it and my body as I bend down into a quick dip.

As is the tradition, the cars launch forward. I quickly stand and inch closer to Trenton's side, turning in a circle to follow the movement of both vehicles.

"Drift donuts," I whisper-laugh. "I could not figure out what the hell they were about to do."

Trenton beams.

Hayes and Crow expertly drift in a tight circle around us, teasing the edges of the crates. My heart pounds like mad knowing that if one of them clip a corner, not only will it mess up their cars, but it'll take Trenton and me down, too.

I live for stuff like this, though. Especially when there's somewhat of a security involved. Trenton being the security in this scenario. If he didn't trust his friends, he wouldn't be up here... and I know he certainly wouldn't allow me to be up here with him. Any "classy" car guy is going to go out of their way to keep their "passenger" safe.

When I pivot around, trying to catch a glimpse of Hayes and Crow's faces while in their element, taking chances and masterfully working their equipment, Trenton grabs my hand and tugs me to his side. I tentatively return his shirt.

He doesn't bother to put it back on, stuffing a corner of it into his back pocket instead. My gaze drifts over his bare chest with appraisal.

Eager to watch the show, he tugs me down to sit next to him, legs dangling off the crates. Me, on the other hand, I tuck my knees up, heels propped on one of the skewed edges.

Hayes and Crow continue to perform drift donuts around us. The alternating sounds of engines revving and the whine of power-steering as they strategically counter-turn fills the otherwise silent and empty lot.

Trenton inches closer to me, his rough jeans brushing against my bare thigh. He leans in, twisting the cap off his water, and whispers over the din. "Tell me you wore those shorts for me." His hand, slightly wet and cool from the water bottle, lands on top of my thigh and inches toward the scraggly strings that hang haphazardly from the bottom hem.

Lord, the way he makes me feel all giddy, happy, and warm.

"Keep touching me like that, and I'll tell you whatever you want to hear."

Trenton's fingers slide beneath the ragged material, only to quickly discover — much like Porter did — that I opted out of underwear.

His teeth nip the lobe of my ear. "I change my mind," he breathes. "Tell me you didn't wear any underwear for me."

"Well, I was expecting to get the ones I left in your car back. They're my favorite pair," I share, scooting closer to the edge, forcing his fingers to find their ultimate aim sooner than he had probably planned.

This doesn't seem to bother or deter him, though. He slips inside me easily as I grip one of the planks behind us. My head falls back and eyes close, throat vibrating over a moan.

"Mmm… well, hate to be the bearer of bad news, but I never promised to bring back all of your clothes, and that particular item is the one I decided to keep."

The squeal of tires on concrete makes my eyes snap open, but instead of losing the euphoria of being strummed on the inside while cars zoom around us, the sound only serves to heighten my body's response.

Trenton twists and curves his fingers toward my G spot as Crow passes, tongue toying with his piercing, tattooed knuckles gripping the wheel in utmost concentration, making me imagine all sorts of other ways he can concentrate and things he can grip.

In a flash, he is gone and Hayes appears in my sightline instead. Unlike Crow, Hayes is not only expertly maneuvering his car, his gaze is also on Trenton and me, a lust like no other coating his otherwise usually sheepish disposition.

Appears I'm not the only one who gets off from a little recklessness; Hayes has been holding back. It seems as though he enjoys a bit of voyeurism. I can't help but wonder in what ways his daredevil nature would translate in the bedroom.

Would he stroke his cock, eyes half-mast and watchful, while Trenton strokes my insides like he's doing now?

Or would he rather exhibit his skills while Trenton is on the receiving end of a pleasure-show?

The concoction of my lucid thoughts and his heated eyes unravels me. Heart accelerating right along with their engines, my pussy walls clench, and I let go:

Of my agenda.

Of my memories.

Of my homelife.

Of my body.

I give myself over completely under the ministrations of Trenton's skilled hand. Wood from the crate splintering my palms, and thighs spread wide, Trenton finger fucks me while two speeding cars create a vortex around us.

Every turn a risk to our safety.

Every turn a promise of release.

Every turn an rpm higher in my body until I stall out.

CHAPTER THIRTY-FOUR

Okay, so perhaps I lumped car guys into a stereotype I shouldn't have. Tonight was fun — too fun. These guys? Just normal guys who like cars and are out to have a little fun on occasion.

After the drift donuts, we all worked together to return the crates to their original spots. The black tire marks creating a circle in the middle of the lot, though… those will be around for a while.

One beer per person ended up being enough for tonight. Even Trenton had one ceremoniously after some prodding by the others. Just for the socialization of it all. Water bottles now in hand, we all sit on the edge of the marina, legs dangling precariously over the depths of the obscure water.

Hayes and Trenton sit on either side of me, Crow next to Trenton. The conversation hadn't left cars since we sat down. Right now the guys are talking about the Trans Am that was in attendance both the night I first showed up at The Crowbar and again tonight.

Well, last night technically, seeing as it's now creeped into the early hours of the next day.

"Seems like an alright kid," Crow says. "High as a kite both times he swung through, though. Far as I can tell he isn't part of a crew. Just wants to be."

When the conversation wanes a bit, I take that opportunity to ask more about their own involvement in a club or crew. "I haven't noticed a decal on your cars. Are you three not a part of something official?"

Come to think of it, I don't remember seeing decals on any of the cars at the small meetup last night.

Heck, maybe if I can at least get a name for one of the clubs in this area I will have something more to further my research.

I still can't bring myself to drop the idea of Trenton, Hayes, and Crow being somehow associated. Even though Crow might not race, with them pulling the type of equipment I've now witnessed firsthand and having the skills they've demonstrated tonight, maybe in the least they know someone involved in the scene.

"We all have decals," Trenton reveals. "They're just small. Bottom right edge of the driver's window. That's where you will find most crew decals around this area…"

Crow clears his throat, and Trenton's words trail off suspiciously.

Pretending I didn't pick up on the evasion, I continue my casual prodding. "Oh, well that explains why I didn't see one right off. What is your club name, and were all the cars at The Crowbar tonight part of the same club?" I ask.

Hayes answers this time, emphasizing the first syllable: "Revelry... and no, none of them were."

Crow pushes off the ledge and stands. "Okay, well... time for me to call it a night," he says, yawning and stretching his arms over his head. A black happy trail peeks out when his shirt lifts.

Since he was my ride here, and I am not entirely sure of their plans for who is driving me to my bike, I follow suit, careful not to look at the water while going through the motion of standing.

Trenton and Hayes join in, and we all make our way toward the vehicles.

"Which of you is the lucky driver who gets to take me back?" I inquire.

Crow jangles his keys in the air. "That would be me. I live on the West End."

Since Trenton and Hayes live in town, which is where we are now, and the West End is past The Crowbar in the opposite direction, that makes sense.

My eyes probe Crow's. "If you don't mind? I can always call my brother to come pick me up."

Lord knows I don't want to do that, but I also don't want these guys thinking I can't handle things myself.

Crow lifts a hand to his mouth, the numbers on his knuckles more visible now under a parking lot light.

A year.

A recent one.

"Tempting," he says.

People with tats usually don't mind sharing the reason behind them, but something about his tattoos sends a skitter of unease along the back of my neck. Something tells me the story behind those tattoos are shared on his time, not on anyone else's.

Hayes walks by on the way to his car and punches Crow in the shoulder. Trenton slips behind me and drags a finger along the bare skin of my lower back en route to his own car.

"Bye," Hayes hollers just before ducking down into his seat and closing the door.

Trenton dips into his car, unrolls the passenger side window, holds out my bundle of clothes, and says, "Text me when you get home safely." This comes with a warning glare shot toward Crow.

I understand what they're doing, and it makes me feel a bit uneasy. I know why Hayes and Trenton left: even though those two and I have something brewing between us, anyone within a close vicinity can feel the uncanny vibration between Crow and me.

It had been present all night in brief glances, unintentional touches, occasional quips. Now that we're alone, the sensation is through the roof. It's… uncomfortable. Unusual. Addictive.

Being alone with him is dangerous. Not dangerous in a stalker type of way, but in a *"I can't trust my behavior around guys like this"* kind of way.

When the only lights are the lot lamps shining down on us like spotlights, and the only sound is the rush of water against concrete, that danger amplifies tenfold.

As though he can feel the same pressure building between us, Crow takes a backward step, and his chest lifts and falls through a tentative breath.

"Look… like I said, I can call my brother… or a rideshare." Proving my willingness to follow through, I dig the phone out of my back pocket and begin the process of finding a local rideshare.

Just as I'm hovering my finger over the search button. Crow clears his throat. "Ah… shit. No… just… get in," he says, opening the passenger side door like a true gentleman. Or, maybe more like a man wanting to get this over with as quickly as possible.

"Um… You sure?"

He rolls his eyes and gestures toward the open door.

I lock my screen and duck inside.

"Thanks," I say under my breath.

Crow grunts and closes the door as soon as my feet are clear of the sill.

CHAPTER THIRTY-FIVE

Silence envelops the ride; not a single word is uttered. A stuffy tension reverberates between us even though nothing had happened. We all had a good time. Something had changed, though, and I am completely clueless as to what.

Just like how I am not one of those girly-girls who screech and tense because of a little speed, I am also not one to worry and fret over a man's broodiness.

Crow throws the car into park, and his fingers tap against the steering wheel, teeth nipping at that piercing again.

I am also not the type to linger and wait while he figures out what hard-ass comment to make. Nor will I make it all cutesy awkward, twist my fingers in my lap, and whisper my undying thanks.

Instead, I open the car door, step out, and close it before curving around to my bike and putting on my helmet.

After a twenty-minute drive in silence, apparently Crow plans to pull the gentleman card and wait to follow me out of the parking lot.

Problem is, I don't want him to. Once I painstakingly shove my clothes and clutch into the much-too-small storage compartment and get adjusted on the seat, I twirl my finger at him, assuming he's watching my progress.

Sure enough he rolls down the window. He still doesn't say anything, simply giving me a raised brow.

"Don't wait for me… I need to send a couple texts and check the map for a different route. Might take a few minutes."

I end the conversation by taking the phone out of my pocket and pretending to instantly become fully immersed in my task.

Out of the corner of my eye, I catch his fingers drumming on the steering wheel. He clears his throat, and I return my attention to him. "If you're not going to let me follow you out, at least take down my number and text me so I know you made it home safe."

A small smile ticks up on the corner of my lips as I look back down to my phone and open my contacts to add a new one for Crow.

He recites the number, and I press save. "You guys good with a group thing?" I ask, figuring it would be easiest to just send the three of them a text at the same time.

Crow pulls a face, shooting me an incredulous look. It takes me a moment longer before I realize why he reacted the way he did. I wiggle my phone at him with an eye roll. "Group text?"

I don't blame him for his mind taking that direction; none of us spoke about what Trenton did to me on the crates in clear sight of everyone in our party. I am not ashamed. Nor will I apologize.

The way his steel-gray eyes periodically trailed over my thighs and between my legs without a bit of contempt for the rest of the evening said all I needed to know about his thoughts on the matter. He enjoyed the show, even if he is too moody to outwardly admit it.

"Oh… right. Yeah. That's fine," he responds.

I pocket my phone for a heartbeat, prop my feet on the foot pegs, and lean back slightly. Crow's throat moves over a thick swallow. "And if I had meant the other type of 'group thing'?" I ask just to make him squirm a bit.

Crow puts his car into reverse but keeps his foot on the brake. "Nah, you three keep that kinky shit to yourselves. I don't need a wingman to get the job done."

He doesn't allow the conversation to carry on, reversing with a two-finger salute and rolling away toward the entrance.

Finally alone, the idea of going home seems less than appealing right now. The past twenty-four hours have been busy, filled with testosterone and mental work. I'm no closer to uncovering the underground street racing scene despite my efforts to make forward progress, and when I get home, I'll be walking through the door with empty hands. That knowledge hovers over me like a thick cloud heavy with the promise of a deluge of pain and disappointment. What is supposed to be my safe haven, has turned into the last place I want to be, period.

What I had said to Crow wasn't completely untrue; instead of going home, I decide a little alone time is in order.

This area supposedly has a nice pier somewhere, yet even during the cruise with Hayes, I had not yet seen it. I type in PCB pier and study the route. It's still on The Strip, just a bit farther west.

* * *

THE PIER IS NICE — noted as the longest fishing pier on The Gulf. Comforting, ambient lighting lines the entire length. There isn't a soul around at this hour. I walk all the way down and rest my forearms on the top railing.

The gulf is pitch dark, aside from the reflections of the lights from high rises and other expensive commercial and residential buildings twinkling against the glass-like surface.

In complete opposition to the marina, the air here is fresher and more organic. Pollution, emissions, and dust from ships doesn't taint the experience.

Standing here in solidarity, accompanied only by my thoughts, a calmness descends over me.

Sometimes those thoughts can be poor company, too, but not tonight.

Tonight, I feel refreshed. Alive. Thankful for my new friends.

Giddy at the thought of these budding relationships — since they appear in the clear of being on the receiving end of Jude and Porter's takeover.

Now that I can move on and take a different route, that is. I will still need to dig up more information — possibly from them. But I feel better knowing they're not the ones I'm betraying.

A newfound optimism stirs within me.

Gazing out into the far distance, into nothing but pure black, I permit thoughts about Dad to stand beside me. To speak of the past in hushed tones.

Not of the night he died — I'm not ready for that yet — but of everything else.

His love for the ocean.

For the industry.

For me.

When I am maxed out on the emotions pulling too tightly on my heartstrings, my blurry gaze falls to my clasped hands — to the string ring around my finger. I brush the pad of my thumb over the fraying material with a smile and amused shake of my head.

Why are you still wearing this? I ask myself, knowing I can't wear it forever. It's a string. It'll get nasty after too long.

For some reason I haven't been able to bring myself to take it off, though. It sticks to my skin much like Trenton sticks in my thoughts — constantly there. Constantly making my belly flip.

A yawn overcomes me, and despite wanting to curl up here and sleep on the edge of the pier, I push off the railing and make my way back. Driving while tired is one of few dangerous risks I'm unwilling to take. Time to get home before my exhaustion messes with my ability to concentrate on the road.

Focus down, I continue to toy with the string around my finger as I take the steps at the pier's entrance. When I round the corner of the welcome station, instead of my bike catching my eye, a gleam of red clashes against the night.

No…

Porter leans against the front side of his car. Waiting.

Fear coils around every muscle in my body. A new fear. One I'm not yet intimate with. Porter had unsettled me a few times in the past, and the recent happenings I had brushed off as nothing more than an aggravation. A hindrance. Until they started happening too frequently and more aggressively with each ensuing instance.

Now… I don't know what to do.

How to act.

What to say.

I have already given him my body without a fight.

Already agreed to keep secrets.

Already proven my commitment to dig up information.

What more does he want from me?

CHAPTER THIRTY-SIX

Before, I would have asked him a number of things about his unexpected appearance: What's wrong? Is Jude okay? What are you doing here? But my tongue seems unable to work.

I can't say anything at all.

As if my body controls my mind and not the other way around, I walk right up to him and cower as though I'm an unruly pet expecting punishment for doing something wrong while he was away.

Or, in my case, while *I* was away.

Did I really do something wrong?

Now I'm not sure.

Maybe I did.

But what?

The back of his hand meets my cheek, and my head slings to the side.

My fight is gone.

Somewhere in the depths of the gulf.

Porter grips my jaw and yanks my face back toward his. The tiniest remaining rebellion inside me timidly tries to peek through, with the simple refusal to lift my gaze. But she cowers again when he hisses, "Look at me."

I obey immediately.

I may not like the direction this has taken, but I can't seem to bounce back. My gaze reaches for his, eyes darting left and right, searching for the guy I grew up knowing first like a sibling, then as a friend, then…

My voice box decides to work, but not by any conscious choice on my part. "I'm trying," I plead.

Mere minutes ago, I was thankful Trenton, Hayes, and Crow were a dead end. Now, I wish they were the right guys just so I can tell Porter some good news. Maybe it would change this anger to excitement. Change my punishment to reward.

"You're doing a hell of a lot more than trying," he spits. "In case you're too daft to know, I am in charge of the books right now. I didn't hire you to whore yourself out for answers." His hand drops from my jaw, and he draws a fingertip over the bare skin of my belly button before dipping a finger under the waistband of my shorts.

No.

Not again.

He tugs my waistband and I stumble forward, crumbling against him. "This tight pussy of yours is mine, something you're apparently also too fucking stupid to know. Now that we've cleared that up, though, maybe your job will be a little easier and you'll be less distract—"

The purr of an engine and crunch of tires over gravel cuts his proclamation short. Out of the corner of

240

my eye, light bounces off a windshield. "There a problem here?"

That voice.

The low, bass pitch that flirts with danger and rebellion.

Crow.

Holy shit.

Head shaking in response to the question, in a silent plea for him to stay out of this, my eyes travel sideways in an attempt to steal a validating glance. Crow doesn't appear in my peripheral, but an inky black Supra does.

My mind wars with whether I should be happy he's here… or terrified.

"There's your answer," Porter grinds out.

"Come again? Sorry, I didn't quite *hear* an answer the first time." The engine cuts off and a door hinges open. My heart swells and aches concurrently.

The sting of my cheek throbs knowing that when Crow leaves there will be more. More of whatever new and surprising things Porter has in store for me.

Porter dips his mouth to my ear. "Tell him."

My tongue has been temperamental since this started, and now is no different. Paralyzed by fear, I can do nothing more than shake my head in dismissal again.

Problem is, this time I am dismissing Porter, and he doesn't like that very much. With a growl of frustration, his finger curls deeper into my waistband, knuckle digging into the soft flesh just beneath.

As though Crow knows a verbal answer isn't going to come, the sound of his door closing tears into my crippling fear. This time, I dare a whole head turn in his direction. He doesn't approach, but simply leans against his car, feet crossed at the ankles. "You're the new guy who showed up uninvited to our meetup last night, right? Porter."

Porter does a double take, only just now recognizing Crow as the guy who had first spoken to him when he and Jude rolled onto the lot. "Look man, this has nothing to do with you. This is between my girlfriend and me. You can leave."

The whites of Crow's eyes appear in the shadows followed by the gleam of teeth when he opens his mouth to say something but closes it again. Once he gets his expression under control, his steely eyes flash like a glint of chrome. Right at me.

My stomach constricts on itself, becoming dead weight inside my body. Again, I shake my head.

Why?

To whom?

Crow, to insist Porter isn't my boyfriend?

Porter, to beg him to drop it so Crow will leave?

Right now, I'm not sure which.

Coming to some sort of conclusion, Crow crosses his arms and pierces Porter with a challenging glare.

"Fine. That her bike over there?" he asks tilting his head minutely in that direction. Porter's nostrils flare and his eyebrows straighten. But that's all the response Crow needs to continue. "Thought so. How about you let her hop on and drive home, then. If she's your girlfriend, I imagine you two can finish this conversation there." He displays his phone. "Or... I can call the police."

A rumble emits from Porter's chest, but his finger finally leaves the waistband of my shorts. I take the opportunity to stagger back and put distance between us, fighting the urge to dust him off my body and hold back a shiver of repulsion.

After what Crow said fully registers, I take off toward my bike. "Wait," he says low, "Porter will leave first." I spin around, continuing toward my bike with small, tentative backward steps. A moment of silence represses the air between the three of us. "Won't you?" he finishes.

Porter and I both gape at him. For some disconcerting reason, however, Porter acquiesces. And when he does, in that precise moment, his silent agreement is the most terrifying thing I have ever experienced where he is concerned.

More terrifying than the sting of knuckles.

More terrifying than the manipulation.

More terrifying than the non-consent.

Porter doesn't back down from a challenge. He doesn't bend to someone else's will. That is precisely why he was always such a valuable resource to my father. He'd help make dealings no one else had the balls to.

This show of compliance will undoubtedly come with a consequence.

When Porter starts his car and his headlights burn bright, disappearing into the vast gulf ahead, I close the distance to my bike. While I put on my helmet, Porter reverses, turns toward the road, and performs a burnout, leaving a plume of white smoke in his wake.

Just as I am about to sling my leg over the seat, Crow pushes off his car and stalks my direction. Knowing full well he is also displeased with me, but suddenly very unsure how that displeasure will translate, every muscle in my body locks tight.

When the terror in my gaze registers, he comes to a dead halt, hands flying up and palms out. "I'm not going to hurt you. Just… don't go yet, okay?"

I blink a few times through my visor, give him a terse nod, and move around my bike to lean against it instead of mounting.

He taps something into his phone, and I yell "Stop!" through the helmet, rushing to unclip and remove it to ensure he hears. "Don't call the police."

"I'm calling Hayes so he can meet us and get the tracker off your phone before you go anywhere," he explains.

"Th—the tracker?" I cover my mouth with the palm of my hand for a second before dropping it limp into my lap. The planted fear from earlier sprouts and grows thick limbs in an instant. "No... He... He wouldn't go that far."

Crow's mouth presses into a line, the piercing burying between his tight lips. "Fine. We'll have Hayes look at it for us and make sure. Will that asshole be at 'home' when you get there tonight?"

I bite my lip and my gaze falls to the ground.

"Do you want to go home?"

My shoulders slump.

"Would you like to take Trenton and Hayes up on their offer?"

My head jerks back up and eyes flash to his.

"I overheard Trenton talking to you at the meetup. Answer my question."

Still fumbling to use my voice, I uncross my arms and ankles and tilt my head to the side. We continue playing this game where he reads and understands my body language like a well-used book. Like he's known me forever and can interpret everything about me.

I definitely don't want to go home. But eventually I'll need to, and whatever Porter has in

245

mind, it will happen regardless. Tonight. Tomorrow. It's just a matter of when.

Unless, I give him exactly what he wants most.

Maybe I should just straight out ask these guys about a racing club. Throw caution to the wind like I probably should have just done to begin with, anonymity be damned.

That is, if there wasn't an unspoken rule against underground street racers discussing details with strangers, no matter their gender or how much fun you have together.

As though I never ran into that dead end to begin with, I'm back to grasping at straws, convincing myself that by getting the information, no matter the outlet, I can reroute any anger and pain that might be awaiting me when I do finally return home.

CHAPTER THIRTY-SEVEN

C row shoves his phone into his back pocket. We remain motionless several feet apart. I am leaning against my bike; he is standing in the middle of the parking lot, arms hung loose at his sides. His shoulders aren't tense, but his hands are. One is curved into a ball, and the fingers on the other twitch slightly.

If it weren't for being subjected to the follow-through of aggressive ticks like that too frequently as of late, perhaps I wouldn't have flinched.

But I do.

And he notices.

The hand that is bunched into a fist loosens and comes to his mouth. His tattooed fingers rub across his jaw and over his chin, eyes darkening as he peers at me from under thick, black lashes.

When his hand drops again, he straightens and says, "I'm fucking pissed, but I'm not going to hit you." He mumbles something, but the words travel to me on the beach breeze nonetheless: "The fuck have I gotten myself in the middle of?"

Even though I haven't known Crow for long, I take his words as a promise and give him a tense nod. "Pissed at... me?" I seek clarity.

"Hell yes I'm pissed at you." His hand clenches again. "When were you planning on telling Hayes and Trenton that you have a boyfriend?" A flash of chrome glints across his steely gaze again. He takes a couple slow steps forward, promising physical caution despite the verbal slash.

Crossing my arms over my chest and lifting my chin, I state, "Because Porter is not my boyfriend." God, this sounds like a high school all over again.

"He seems to think so." More steps forward, this time doubled. "The way he was looking at you... That kind of look usually means more than just friends." The next time he progresses forward, we meet toe to toe. "That kind of look tells me he's had a piece and wants more."

My heart rate triples, breathing increases, and a tremor moves down my arms and into my hands. How dare he pry and judge. Anger and frustration make my vision shake. Pulling in a deep breath, I drop my gaze to the pavement. Voice trembling, I explain through mumbled words, "Not that it's any of your damn business, but he *was* my boyfriend. He *has* had a piece of this. Several times."

Tone low and menacing, Crow dips his head down to recapture my focus. "He's not only getting in your pants" — he drags a finger across my stomach, then lifts it and taps my temple — "he's getting in your head, too."

His correct assessment only serves to worsen my budding anger. At this rate, those tremors... the wavering vision... will need an outlet. If I'm not careful, that outlet will undoubtedly be in the form of embarrassing angry tears.

Lost in an attempt to control the way I'm spiraling, the feel of Crow's fingers as they grip my jaw, hard and pressing, shocks the anger right out of me, immediately turning it into dread.

Not a dread lending toward wondering if he'll break his promise and prove he's no better — no different — than Porter.

A dread that he won't break that promise. But, rather, further prove the very first assessment I made of him: he is the brooding, dangerous type. The type that, when touching me like this — rough with the promise of safety — I spiral out of control in a completely different way.

He squeezes my jaw, angling my face upward, silently demanding I look at him. Instead of giving him what he wants, instead of lifting my gaze, my lashes flutter, eyes seeking out anything but his while his hand sears my skin.

The same sear that now travels down my neck and blooms across my chest.

When my eyes do finally lock on something, the dread consumes me completely. That damn lip ring.

Tension swirls around us, so thick I swear if I take in a deep breath it'll seize my lungs like the smoke from burning rubber.

When his tongue snakes out and gives it a quick flick, I realize he'd been tracking my eyes.

Watching. Waiting to see where they would land.

Assessing.

Judging.

Assuming.

His lips tick, and he gives my face a looser, gentler jostle this time. "Ah," he says, and I hyper-focus on the way his mouth moves. "See. Your silence did nothing to prove me wrong. You're one of those women who enjoy being toyed with. Is that why you let him fuck you?" With his free hand he once again reminds me what types of fucking he's referring to. His fingertip flicks my hip before rising to tap my temple.

My teasing anger flares, and my eyes flash up to his, locking there. Resolute.

Problem is, he's right.

What's worse, he knows it.

The tick of his mouth turns into a smirk.

For a second, his hand tightens before loosening and skimming his fingertips over my jaw where he'd been pressing. The smirk fades, and his gaze becomes just as resolute as mine. Seems he's not done playing judge, though — "Trouble is, you've gotten yourself into a situation where it started out fun and went downhill before you could label what was happening. Now, you don't know how to get out." — and getting it right. Mostly.

Silence is my only friend right now. Silence…

…and the arrival of Hayes.

Fingers still hot against my skin, Crow's gaze falls to my mouth, and he drags his thumb slowly along my bottom lip, dropping his voice to a whisper. Once again, as if he has exclusive access to who I am down to my very soul, he states, "Do all the mind and cock fucking you want, Remi. But leave Hayes and Trenton out of it. Fuck with my friends, and we're going to have problems."

His hand abandons my face, loops around my back, slides into my back pocket, and pulls out my phone.

That dread returns.

The unpleasant one.

Debilitating.

Consuming.

Heart-wrenching.

Crow sees past my sloppy facade. Past the lies. He just can't put a finger on what I'm lying about. He almost hit the nail on the head, minus the part that I don't know how to get out of this mess. I know… At least I think I do. I'm just struggling to come to terms with the consequences of what it'll take.

Saving myself… means betraying them.

CHAPTER THIRTY-EIGHT

"**D**amn, you got here fast," Crow hollers over his shoulder, hands leaving my face just as quickly as he had put them there.

"Never went home," Hayes responds, getting out of his car and closing the door.

"Clearly." Crow flicks a glance at me and back to Hayes.

"So…" Hayes shoots me a look and rubs the back of his neck. "What's up?"

Crow holds out my phone. Hayes takes it without question, twisting it in his hand. "Check her for a tail or whatever it's called. Disable it or whatever the hell needs to be done to make sure she's not being tracked."

Clearly, Crow isn't the tech-savvy one of the bunch.

Hayes's mouth curves into a small frown as his attention moves from Crow then over Crow's shoulder to me.

Tired of the judgment — tired of feeling like the dupe in this entire ordeal — I don't have it in me to keep my eyes and head up. They drop, hard and cold to the ground.

Footsteps approach until four feet are in my periphery. My gaze sneaks a peek upward from under my eyelashes. Crow plays with his lip ring, the bottom of his tongue swiping across it as he watches Hayes swipe deft fingers across the device.

The screen reflects in Hayes's glasses, a bright-white light blocking his eyes.

Curiosity overpowers my natural urge to stay disconnected and shut down. My head rises and my focus tunes into his facial expressions.

His eyebrows are flattened in concentration but everything else pretty much relaxed. That is until the reflective bright-white changes to black, his thumb hovers above the screen, and his gaze reaches over the rim of his glasses. "Not only is your location being tracked, but so are your messages and calls, too. I have a phone number here that the information is being routed to:" — Hayes announces the phone number one digit at a time, and as each falls from his mouth, I crumble a little more. By the last number, I'm on the ground, back pressed uncomfortably against my bike, knees tucked to my chin, arms squeezing around my shins.

Tears pour down my face.

Air refuses to enter my lungs as I gulp and gasp interchangeably.

"Th-that's not possible," I heave. "H-he's dead. Dad is dead. Th-that's his number."

Hayes drops to his haunches in front of me. Hand cupping my face, he says, "The line is active. Did you or your brother deactivate the number after his death?"

"I-I don't know. P—" I realize the coincidence a heartbeat after the first sound falls from my lips. Porter was in charge of handling all that, having been given the Power of Attorney right before Dad's last breath in the hospital.

Crow was right.

Again, I was wrong — blind. Porter has been tracking me. My eyes dart up to Crow. He's not smirking, not smug. He simply probes me with a knowing stare and taps his temple.

Hayes falls to his knees and scoots around me. Ducking his head under my bike, his hand runs along the underbelly.

He then stands, presses on my phone's built-in flashlight and walks around to the other side where the light from the parking lot lamp doesn't quite reach.

Too weak and drained to get up yet, I quietly wait. My attention floats up to Crow again. He's watching me with a gaze far too perceptive. His teeth capture his lip ring and he scrubs a hand down his face. The longer he looks down at me, despite the horrifying revelation that I'm being tracked, the more that fiery inferno whorls around us, attempting to drag us into nonreturnable depths.

As though he has little to no control of his body, he steps forward with furrowed eyebrows and sits in front of me, knees up, tattooed knuckles dangling between them. "When something happens in this area, it becomes my business. Once he drove onto the lot at The Crowbar, his business became mine. But… so did yours. Do you need help?" He stresses the word help, and a similar conversation with Trenton at the meetup returns to my forethoughts.

Crow isn't asking me if I want him to get the law involved; he's asking if he or any of his friends need to do something about this.

My eyes flare open, and I shake my head emphatically.

"I thought as much. If he keeps showing out in public, you won't be able to protect him forever."

It's not him I'm trying to protect…

Right now, though, as far as I know Jude isn't on their radar seeing as Porter handled the strut and conversation at the meetup. Plus, no one has seen Jude in his own car.

My thoughts are thwarted when Hayes returns and holds out his hand toward Crow. Crow displays his palm. Hayes drops something into the center.

Crow then holds up a small device between his thumb and forefinger. "Your phone wasn't the only thing being tracked," he reveals, tossing a small device in the air and catching it in his palm, wrapping his fingers around the tiny piece and enclosing it inside a tight fist.

He pushes off the ground and marches off toward the pier. Once over the water, he throws the tracker into the deep.

"Is it safe for you to go home?" Hayes asks, holding a hand out to help me up.

Standing, I dust the gritty pieces of asphalt off my palms. But I don't have a helpful answer to give. A shrug is all I can manage.

I don't know.

Feeling unsafe in my own home is a new thing.

How far Porter has pushed lately is a new thing.

Doing Lance Industries' dirty work is a new thing.

"I was thinking maybe I could stay with you and Trenton tonight... if the offer still stands? Let all of this settle. Figure out what I'm going to do." I hate sounding so needy. So dependent.

"Yeah." He lifts his hand to the back of his neck. A warm, barely-there smile graces his lips. "Maybe have a couple drinks, get your mind on something else for a while?"

A pent-up breath leaves my lungs. "A distraction? Yes, please."

Best offer I've received... in a week.

CHAPTER THIRTY-NINE

W ord on the street there's the makings of a new crew in town. Someone throwing around terms and hints to a few of the local key automotive players.

When the red Mustang pulled up to our crew-leader and new-members meetup, I wasn't entirely caught off guard. After running it by both Hayes and Trenton and learning that he didn't come by the date, time, and location because of a golden ticket, though? Now that shit, on the other hand, is concerning.

Sure, we were meeting in public along a major road. Anyone driving past interested in cars could've pulled through out of curiosity. Fine.

That isn't how it happened, though. This guy — Porter, or whoever the hell it was driving what I assume is his car at the time — turned in as if The Crowbar was the intended destination. No slow drive by, assessing an interesting situation. No passing only to turn around and double back out of curiosity.

Before my crew left to hit the marina, I asked a few of the other crew leaders about both the red Mustang and the rumor of a new crew. No one recognized them — the guys, the car, or the rumor.

Aside from the new guy with the Trans Am and these tools with the red 'Stang, Remi was the only new attendee. It would take a fucking idiot to not piece two and two together, especially with the way she occasionally throws around street terms like she's been around the block several times.

Sent up too many damn red flags to count.

My eyes roll up to the roof of my car.

Yeah, seems she has no trouble taking a spin around the block... in more ways than one. Maybe I should go ahead and tap it before Trenton gets in too deep. Take my turn.

Just thinking about it makes my dick hard, and I have to shift in my seat to relieve some of the pressure. I might not be into that tag team shit, but I have nothing against taking a turn.

With that persistent pull between us, it's a miracle I haven't pounced already. Probably would've if it weren't for Trenton and Hayes being all pussy-whipped... and for the brutally honest fact that I don't trust her. At all.

But the way she clammed right up when Porter rolled to a stop a few yards from her at the meetup, that fear and trepidation... I felt that shit in my veins. I'd seen body language like that too many times in Hayes's sister's eyes. Back in the days when he'd call me to come take her somewhere until his dad chilled the fuck down or passed out, toe up — whichever came first.

When we parted ways tonight, I had zero intention of leaving her to drive off on her own. I wasn't sure whether that was because of the lack of trust or because I saw too many nonverbal cues that reminded me of when Nikki was silently pleading for help everywhere she went and within every interaction, yet everyone around her was blind to the signs.

All I knew is I was determined to find out. I'd watched from across the street, thankful for my black car and the moonless night so she couldn't see as I studied her strolling down the pier. Every inch of her confidence and joviality from tonight had drained away, replaced by drooping shoulders, the shuffling of feet, and downcast eyes.

I was about to leave — guilt eating me up that I was so untrusting when she clearly just wasn't ready to go home yet — but then that damn Mustang appeared.

At first, I silently raged, slamming my palm against the wheel as the 'Stang's arrival proved I was right about her involvement. But when he cut the lights, killed the engine, and coasted silently into the parking lot, ice licked down my spine. Something was very, very wrong with this situation.

Once in the parking lot, he managed to maneuver to a section in the only sliver of black between lamps. Watching. Waiting.

Unknowingly filling me with so much more damn anger that I was seeing a red deeper than the color of his fucking car.

And when she left the pier and he touched her? Grabbing her in a way absolutely no one should be grabbed? I was starting my car and rolling that way before I could convince myself otherwise. Before I could knock common sense into my own mind. Before I could logically stop and leave well enough alone.

Even after Hayes arrived, the situation was somewhat diffused, and light was shed on how this fuck-twit is screwing with her and she needs to to be snapped into the reality of her situation before getting so lost it consumes her. Even after that I found myself caring way more than I ever intended.

On the "bright side" it also shed light on why the hell this Porter guy showed up uninvited to our meetup. He'd tracked her there.

Where else had he discovered she'd been?
Every-fucking-where, that's where.

Impatience waning by the second as my thoughts get carried away with the entire situation again, I lean out of my window and holler at her and Hayes. They hadn't stopped talking since I stormed off, thrown the tracker into the gulf, and returned to my car, ready to get the hell out of here.

Hayes gives me a one-finger salute, and I return the kindness. But the back and forth is enough to kick them into motion. She puts on her helmet and mounts her bike.

Hayes hops into his car, and in a matter of a few more seconds, the three of us are lined up side by side. Hayes pulls out first, then Remi, then me.

The bluetooth in my car rings. With the push of a button, I answer the call. "Yeah?"

"You staying at our place tonight?" Hayes asks.

I groan and run a hand down my face before dropping it back onto the shifter to switch gears. "Yeah, guess I am."

Hayes attempts to muffle a laugh, but it still comes through loud and clear. "The fuck is so funny HazerBeam?" I stress his ridiculous screen name.

"Play hard to get, Crow. Chicks dig that shit." He throws back what I'd said to Trenton the night this woman single-handedly turned their worlds upside down.

"Hey, I'm not the one falling at her feet, proposing marriage, finger fucking her in a public location, and giving her keys to move in. That's on you two."

"Might as well be. That shit between you two is hotter than tires after a burnout competition. If I were

262

you, I wouldn't be waiting too long to take a closer look before something explodes. Speaking of taking a look… enjoying the view?

"Aren't you fucking hilarious tonight."

For the record, I've been trying to avoid said "view."

The way her shorts dip low in the back, teasingly close to showing her ass.

The bare strip of skin between said ass and shirt.

The swells of her thighs on either side of the seat.

The grip and twist of her hands.

No thanks to Hayes, I'm reminded of all these little details and my eyes cannot fucking stop looking. Everything about her is the very reason why the term *brain fade* ever came to exist.

And brain fade is the very reason why this damn fire between us needs to be snuffed out… and fast.

"Heads up." Hayes's voice — less chipper than just a few seconds ago — tears through my dissolving concentration. The scene around me sharpens back into focus.

"Fuck, where'd he come from?" The red Mustang weaves tightly within the lane and puts on a light show behind me, brights flashing. "Aww, hell no. Fucking trouble. That's what she is. You realize this, right?"

"From my vantage point, the tool behind you is the problem. Not her."

If I could verbally roll my eyes, I would. "Huh. Making you stupid already, I see."

Hayes huffs.

My eyes alternate from rearview mirror to Remi and back again.

"Do you—"

"Let me just ride this out for a minute. See what he thinks is about to happen." One of these days, I'll race again. Today is not that day, though. Hayes knows this better than anyone. To the point where, if it came down to it, he would run the race for me.

"About to find out," Hayes responds.

There's a stale green traffic light about five hundred feet ahead.

"See if you can get her to run it," I state.

"No fucking way," he responds. "You get her to run it. I'll fall back."

My hands leave the wheel and I push them into my temples, bunching up hair between my fingers before dropping them to the wheel again. "Fuck. Fuck. Fuck. Okay… Yeah… Thanks."

"You can thank me later."

Hayes taps his brakes and moves toward Remi's left. I speed up until I'm at her right side and we've hemmed her between lanes. When her head turns toward me, my heart and stomach clench; her eyes are blood red, her helmet collecting puddles of tears. The signal turns yellow. I snap my gaze to the light, back at her, and bounce my eyebrows. Those dark brown eyelashes flutter and she gives me a minute, but sharp, nod.

I accelerate and pull in front of her, eyes seeking any signs of traffic in the intersection before checking my mirrors to see if she's following. When her headlight appears in my passenger's side window, her bike close to my bumper, I let out a sigh of relief. We clear the signal just as it's turning red.

After Hayes had fallen back, he'd matched Porter's weaving — right for left, tit for tat — blocking him from being able to speed up and catch Remi and me. A smirk tugs at my mouth when Hayes stops at the intersection, forcing Porter to stop, too.

The Mustang's lights appear around the driver's side of the Bimmer, lining up beside him to stage for a dig.

A curve blocks the view, and my focus returns back to the bike behind me just in time to witness Remi decelerate.

No.

Goddammit.

She makes a sharp u-turn, and before I change my mind, I drift into one, back tires swerving as I counter-turn to make the adjustment and head in pursuit of the woman who I pegged as trouble from the start and continues to prove me right.

She stops a ways down on the side of the road, ready for the show. I stop far enough away so that I'm not close enough to jump out and knock some damn sense into her.

Truth be told, I didn't much like leaving Hayes anyway. At least this way, I can see what's going on and be able to do something if things take a turn for the worse.

Guess she probably feels the same way.

What I can't figure out, though, is whose side she is on.

CHAPTER FORTY

Crow might not ever know how thankful I was for him the moment he pulled alongside me and dragged me out of the pits of my fear and despair with just a simple gesture.

But it was also enough to remind me that, if it weren't for me, Hayes and Crow wouldn't be taking risks to keep me safe. To defend my honor.

Just before the light turns green, the nose of Porter's Mustang rises, proving the hint of a foul start. Surprise. Even so, Hayes takes the lead right away.

Problem is, I've been a passenger in Porter's Mustang enough times to know that he runs them down closer to the end.

And to also know that he plays dirty. Porter has been known to clip cars in the past, and like hell am I going to let him get away with that this time. If I play things just right, I can easily make it look like I'm helping him, not Hayes.

As soon as they are feet from passing, I open the throttle, turn in behind them and split the lane.

Both men narrow glares at me from either side as they each let up ever so slightly on the gas. I look at Hayes and close my eyes just long enough to hopefully remind him of the closed-eyed, intuitive lesson he'd given me earlier.

We haven't known each other for long, and there's absolutely no reason for him to trust me, but I silently plead that he does. For now.

He presses his lips together and returns his focus to the road ahead, that unwavering concentration he'd displayed at the marina kicking in.

Then my attention moves to Porter.

"What the fuck are you doing, Remi? Get your ass home where you belong and leave the streets to the men."

Oh ho ho ho.

No he just didn't.

Maybe this will make things worse.

Maybe I'll regret doing it.

But enough is enough.

If I can make this work to where he doesn't immediately place the blame on me, maybe a temporary end will be put to the madness.

When Crow and I had taken the turn ahead, I studied every single detail and discovered a small cut-through behind a shop on the bend of the curve.

The lane Porter is in ends in a merge, but just like the lacking sidewalks, apparently they didn't deem it necessary to put up a "lane ends" sign. I also know Porter is experienced enough to be able to drift and slide to a last minute stop without rolling.

The main, uneducated guess I'm taking here is that Hayes knows this street like the back of his hand, and Porter knows this street about as well as he apparently knows the extent of my driving skills.

See, that's the thing about racing.

Every decision is a chance taken. Every rpm a risk.

I speed up more and easily take the lead.

Knowing what I know about what Hayes has under the hood, and how Porter would undoubtedly clip Hayes's car intentionally at the curve when he runs out of road, I take matters into my own hands.

As soon as I'm far enough ahead to safely take the lane in front of Porter, I do just that. Acting as a pace car, if you will. A guide.

As fucked up as Porter is, I know he'd draw a hard line at causing me to wreck. Little does he know, that's not a line I won't cross where he is concerned.

By pulling in front of him and speeding up, he should assume I'm on his side. Once it's established that I don't intend to fall back again, the sound of revving engines filters through my helmet. They're back at it, from a roll this time. The customary three honks belt out in rapid succession.

From here on, I'm blind to everything behind me. A risk like this needs full concentration. I reach out and collapse my mirrors, not trusting myself to refrain from checking on their progress.

Leaning my body in tighter against the tank, I fixate on the upcoming cut-through.

With a single-minded focus, I whip into that alleyway, Porter on my ass, and ride through until I'm on the other side of the curve.

I come to a quick stop, heart pounding, and twist my body to look over my shoulder. Not a five count later, the squeal of tires meets my ear followed by the boom that indicates impact.

Nausea taking over, chest rising and falling, I watch the bend. Waiting.

A flash of purple under a flickering streetlight catches my eye as Hayes rounds the corner. It takes every bit of physical control not to collapse and fall off my bike into a ball onto the ground.

I hold my arm up, shaking, at a 90-degree angle and fist my hand in the signal requesting Hayes to stop.

Red brake lights flash behind him, intermingling with the bright whites of an approaching black car. Another wave of relief flushes through me.

Hayes pulls up as close as he can, and the words tumble out of my mouth almost too soon. "How bad is it?"

"He should be fine. His car won't be, though." Hayes rubs the back of his neck, a small grin slowly curving up his lips, but it's mixed with something else. A deep-rooted sadness? "Fair warning, Crow might be a bit of a mess when we get safely inside the house."

"Oh… okay."

Crow pulls up on Hayes's passenger side. "Time to fly. Someone called the cops." His eyes are wild, hands clenched on his steering wheel, teeth worrying his piercing.

CHAPTER FORTY-ONE

Hayes was right. As soon as we walk into the house, Crow breaks down. Goosebumps travel from the base of my skull down my spine to my tailbone as he collapses onto the couch and buries his head between his hands, fingers twisting into his hair. His shoulders and upper back heave through strained breaths.

Knowing Crow better than I do, Hayes and Trenton leave him alone to work through the silent agony on his own.

Trenton grabs a beer, opens it, and hands it to me. "You deserve a drink."

"Do I?" Heart still going a mile a minute with no sign of slowing anytime soon, I accept the proffered beverage. "Is... is he going to be okay?" Every heaving breath Crow takes seems to travel to me, and my body responds in kind. A shared panic, even if mine is saturated with adrenaline.

Hayes rubs the back of his neck, and he and Trenton share one of those knowing looks. "Yeah, he just needs to blow off a little steam," Hayes explains.

Trenton drops his voice to elaborate, "Impromptu street races are sorta a sensitive topic for him. Especially ones that end in a collision." By this point, I realize Hayes must've called Trenton on the way back and briefed him.

Dropping the topic of Crow's upset, Hayes states, "We've already had enough proof that you know a thing or two about vehicles... but seeing you drive like that? Splitting lanes and using the topography to your benefit? Sure was fun to watch."

Hayes slinks away and wrangles Crow's cell phone out of his pocket. Trenton wraps an arm around my waist and buries his nose in the hair at my neck. That damn adrenaline has every nerve in my body extra sensitive.

It is because of this feeling — the rush — that racing exists. And that thrill lingers.

"He records everything," Hayes explains on his return. "Incriminating evidence and all that," he adds with a wink.

Hayes fingers the phone and holds it out, displaying a shaky video of Hayes, Porter, and me zooming past. I watch in third-person as I swerved off the road onto the cutoff at the last minute, Hayes slammed on his brakes, and Porter kept moving ahead. He'd drifted to a stop, just as I'd expected he would, but slid sideways into a light pole. "She straight stalkered him," Hayes says to Trenton, laughing.

Is it terrible that the only thing that worries me about the outcome is that whatever the cost of the damage he'd done would come from the funds we're trying so hard to protect? To increase?

Not whether Porter is hurt.

Not if someone had seen my involvement.

Not that I'd been recorded.

"Stalkered?" I ask, surprisingly not familiar with the term.

Hayes looks up from the screen and adjusts his glasses with a knuckle. "Eh, online racing lingo for when someone causes a wreck intentionally."

Trenton groans against my neck, and the vibration sends a shiver throughout my body. "A girl who plays dirty… I like it."

Hayes returns to Crow, and Trenton spins me toward him, pressing our bodies flush. He smushes our noses together, eyes sparkling in mischief. I roll my eyes at him and he chuckles. "I am all for being friends," he says, voice dripping with a heat friends typically don't speak with, "but I'm thinking we might need to make it a long-distance thing. You know, like pen pals or something." He draws his face back, adding the proper amount of distance so we can at least focus our vision on each other.

I dip my voice low, high on the rush, and revved up on a new-found confidence. "What if I've changed my mind?"

Trenton's eyebrows curve inward and he runs a finger near the corner of my mouth, removing a piece of hair that had attached to my lip. "Tell me what to do to make that happen," he says as that warm, sepia gaze floats up to mine.

My pulse thuds relentlessly in my ears. "Tell me why both you and your best friend seem to have no trouble sharing my affections."

Really, Remi? That's what you want to know?

How about, "Tell me if you are part of the local underground street racing club?"

Instead, my body finds the idea of working off this adrenaline in the most primalistic way possible preferable — if the heat and dampness pooling between my legs are any indicator.

I peek over my shoulder. Hayes has found a spot on the couch, forearms perched on top of his thighs, hands dangling between as he speaks in a hushed tone with Crow.

As though he can sense my curious gaze, his attention moves over his shoulder and meets mine briefly before returning to Crow.

"That's what best friends are for," Trenton whispers, drawing warm, damp lips along the shape of my ear. My eyes close and neck lengthens, bending to the side for more.

A mix between a groan and a moan trickles past my lips. "Are you trying to take advantage of me when I'm high on adrenaline and vulnerable because I just aided and abetted my ex's wreck?"

Trenton adds his other arm around my waist and draws me in even tighter. "Yep. Don't turn me down. It'll break my heart. True story."

A laugh lodges in my chest. Any hint of trepidation my subconscious might have been hanging on to gushes like a popped water balloon. The way this man makes me feel so comfortable — the way he makes me so easily trust him, burns something inside me.

God I want him.

And the fact that I want him more than just as a bedmate slams so hard into me, the force draws me back and out of his arms.

I bounce against something hard and warm behind me. This time, however, I don't bother to retreat. My eyes close, and I whisper, "We really need to stop bumping into each other like this."

Hayes's awkward chuckle meets my ears and his arms come around my waist. "Do we?" he asks, squeezing lightly. Seems I'm not the only one being drip-fed from a bag of adrenaline. It's no wonder he is a risk taker, that adrenaline very nearly turns him into someone else entirely.

Guards and awkwardness dropped, Hayes comes out of his shell completely. I like it.

My phone rings — a sound I seldom hear when most people simply text — and we all jolt to attention.

Even Crow, who is up on his feet instantly, stumbling toward us before the second ring completes.

I pull the phone from my pocket, eyes meeting each of the guys now craning their necks to peek at the screen.

"Who is it?" Crow asks.

My gaze drops to the phone, and I let out a constrictive breath. "It's my brother."

The postures of all three men immediately loosen.

Crow leans against the back of the couch, crossing his arms over his chest. Hayes removes the still untouched beer from my hand. Trenton takes my now-damp hand, weaves our fingers together, and gives me an encouraging squeeze.

I press the answer button with my thumb, hold the phone up to my ear, and attempt to sound as neutral and normal as possible. "Hey!"

"Hey, Remi." Jude's greeting isn't nearly as peppy as mine.

"Everything okay?" I ask, dropping my voice in concern.

The next words out of Jude's mouth are delivered with a tremble to his voice that I seldom hear. "Porter got into a wreck."

Fearing the worst, a thick sludge of trepidation slowly spreads through me. Yet, my mind and heart struggle in earnest with how to respond. Silence buzzes over the speaker.

What if it's worse than what Hayes said?

Do I want him to be okay?

Can I handle the guilt if he's not?

Trenton squeezes my hand again, providing me with a much-needed lifeline. "I-is he okay?" I finally ask.

Jude lets out a shaky breath. "Yeah. He's fine. Totaled his car, though. The hospital is keeping him overnight as a safety precaution."

I let out a quiet gasp, but for some sick, sick reason, it begins to morph into a laugh. The first squeak is all that comes out before a hand wraps around from behind me and covers my mouth.

Since I can't look backward with the way Hayes has his arm over my shoulder, my eyes land on Crow instead. His knuckled fingers are over his mouth, cupping his jaw, little crow's feet frame his eyes. When our gazes lock only a few heartbeats pass before he breaks the sudden, and inappropriately timed, sizzle of connection by dropping his gaze.

When I feel confident that the percolating giggles are under control, I wrap my fingers around the hand at my mouth and tug it down.

"Holy shit," I breathe. "That..."

"Yeah, I'm just glad he's okay."

"I-I met some friends and have been hanging out with them all night, figured I'd just stay over here since it's so late and I'm getting tired. But, I can come home, if you need company? Or-or if you think Porter—"

"Nah. I just wanted to let you know. You have fun. I'd rather you in a bed than riding if you're tired anyway."

I don't know what I was going to say where Porter was concerned, but Jude cutting me off saved me from making any offers begrudgingly. "Okay. But if you change your mind, please call. Promise?"

"Promise…" The inflection of the word trails toward the end, but after a breath he speaks up again, "Remi?"

"Yeah?"

"When Porter called and mentioned a wreck, I-I thought he was going to say it was you." Jude's voice catches. "I couldn't stand. Couldn't breathe. It was like—" he stops there, cutting short the painful memory of receiving news of our father's death.

My heart leaps off an invisible cliff edge and crumbles to pieces at the bottom. "Oh, Jude. I'm so sorry."

"Nothing to be sorry about." Jude gives a weak chuckle. "I know I don't say it often enough… but I love you."

Wetness pricks at my eyes. "I love you, too."

Jude cuts the line before either of us can get any sappier.

When my phone hand drops to my side, Trenton holds up my still-untouched beer. "So, how about that drink?" I more than gladly accept, wrapping my fingers around the glass.

What Jude doesn't know is that not only was I there tonight, witness and accomplice to Porter's accident, but I was there on the night of my father's death, too.

As a witness… and an accomplice…

The only difference is that one was intentional.

CHAPTER FORTY-TWO

Hayes

Half a beer down, she whips toward me and aims the top of her bottle at me accusingly. "So, you guys do race, then."

It's not a question. She had a front row seat to how easily Crow and I controlled the situation with Porter.

Well, when *she* wasn't controlling it, that is.

My eyes catch on Crow for a second. "Never denied it," I respond, rubbing the back of my neck.

She then turns to Trenton. "How about you? I haven't asked you yet."

"Yeah, I race."

Crow audibly huffs at Trenton's confession, shoving his hands into his pockets. The fire that tends to burn between Remi and Crow lights up when her interrogation moves on to him.

Crow rubs a hand across his jaw. "You already asked, and I already answered."

"Guess that means I'm asking the wrong question, then." She pins him with a glare. He straightens, removes his hands from his pockets, and crosses them over his chest instead. All bulging tattoos and jaw clenched. "Ask then."

Ah fuck.

"Street or strip?" she boldly inquires.

Double fuck.

Crow steps toward her and Trenton slips between them.

I move to Crow's side while Trenton works his charms to redirect her focus. When I peer over my shoulder, he's already pulling her toward his — no, my — bedroom.

Triple fuck.

Before my thoughts can drift to the type of activity those two being in my bedroom might lead to later, I return my attention to Crow. The short distraction was enough; before I can react, I'm stumbling backward from a forceful shove.

"So... what? We just spill all our secrets because some hot piece of ass simply asks?" Crow grinds out.

"Come on, man." I hold my hands up in defense. "No one is spilling secrets. She has been piecing things together on her own. Don't you think she proved herself worthy of some answers tonight, though?"

Crow shakes his head emphatically. "No. Nuh uh. Something underhanded is going on, and you and Trenton can't see past her thighs."

My hands drop, and they ball at my sides. Crow's gaze follows the motion, narrowing a glare at the threat. "Oh... so that is how this is going to play out? Okay. Fine. I'll make you a deal. If you trust her so much, go ahead and give her a golden ticket to the upcoming non-cash meet — make her believe it's the one that counts. Prove me wrong."

"You want to set her up?"

"Fuck yes I do. You know I don't play these games, Hayes. I'm not risking the club over a hot piece of ass who rides a motorcycle. Girls like her get racers killed. Tonight, case in point."

CHAPTER FORTY-THREE

Remi

High on adrenaline and relieved my recent biggest obstacle is alive in a hospital room, I somehow couldn't hold back any longer. With what had just happened between Crow, Hayes, and me, the moment seemed prime.

Until it didn't.

I had worked up so much courage to flat out ask, only to be dismissed. Being on the receiving end of Crow's hackles rising made my confidence deflate.

Trenton removing me from the situation was well-timed.

Ironically, though, this time I wasn't asking for Porter or Jude's benefit... I was asking for myself. A gift amid the torture I had been through since this charade began. Sure, the response might kill two birds with one stone, but right now, I am no longer worried about infiltrating or recruiting. I want to know what these guys are involved in... and I want to be part of it.

My eyes scan Hayes's room. If I thought Jude's tech was impressive, I was wrong; Jude's setup dims in comparison. Hayes has so much equipment, the entire room is bathed in an electronic glow. And his signature color is purple, much like the purple of the abstract paint design on his car.

Computers and devices aren't the only type of equipment, though; in the corner of the room to the left is a weight bench, strategically placed beside an old-school style stereo system.

Trenton sits on the corner of the bed closest to the door, grabs my wrist, and tugs me between his legs. Head tilted back, he reaches up and cups the side of my face. "So, the ex-boyfriend with the Mustang that you mentioned the night we met. That was him, and he's the 'friend' living with you and your brother?" His fingertips ghost over the mark on my face, now probably even redder than earlier since a number of hours have allowed it to set. "And... from what I am piecing together, he's also the one doing this to you?"

Still trying to defend Jude and what small portion of Lance Industries he and Porter have transferred here, I inch backward, lifting my own hand up to my cheek when Trenton's falls away.

"I-it's not always like this. He... he cares about me. You know? Maybe this'll be enough to make him stop. Knock some sense into him."

Oh my God. Seriously, Remi? Listen to what you're saying.

Trenton buys my pathetic excuses about as much as I do. Eyebrows netting together, he says, "You're smarter than that."

My shoulders curve inward, and he lifts his other hand to cup the opposite side of my face. Then, he pulls me down to him and brushes his lips against mine. "This… is what it feels like when someone cares about you." My legs wobble, and I ease myself onto his lap, balancing on one of his knees to keep from falling to the floor. "Don't let him trick you into believing it's supposed to feel like anything else."

Had I? Had he pulled me under far enough to drown in the belief that was all I'd ever be worthy of receiving? That and one-night stands?

One thing is for sure, under his rule, I sure wouldn't dare try seeking out anything more. "I don't know what to do…" I whisper from deep in the recesses of my aching heart.

"One day at a time, Remi. Starting with tonight."

My eyebrow rises and I chuckle, grasping at humor to lighten the haunting direction this conversation is taking. "Are you just trying to get me into bed again?"

"Always," he states, dropping his palm from my cheek and wrapping it around my hand instead. Lifting my fingers up, he studies the still-existing string ring.

"Want to tell me why you haven't taken this off yet?" he asks, placing a light kiss over it.

"I like it. You. Here." I wave my opposite hand, indicating the house in general.

Of course, he easily volleys back, "Hayes's room?"

"The whole house... though, this is pretty impressive, too." Now it's my turn to ask questions again; maybe this one won't get me into more trouble. Or maybe it will. "Want to tell me why you brought me in here instead of *your* room?"

His hands move to around my waist, fingers skating along the bare section of my lower back. "It would take an idiot not to feel the connection between you and Hayes. Crow, too, but he's more... traditional." Trenton rolls his eyes playfully at the description for Crow before shrugging and finishing his answer. "Plus, I want to see where this thing with you and Hayes goes. With the three of us."

My lips part on a quiet gasp.

So... I wasn't just imagining this uncanny triangle.

"W-what about Hayes..." I work out after a thick swallow. "Does he want to see where this thing is going, too?"

"Yeah. Definitely."

"And it doesn't bother you?"

"No. Would it bother you if I admitted that we'd done this before? Shared a woman in bed, I mean. Not the 'feelings' part. That element is new." He chuckles a little, and his typically confident gaze drops for an instant before returning again.

Both the question and his admittance of having feelings about me give me pause. One, because he's so brutally honest it almost hurts. Two, because… for some reason it does kinda bother me. The sharing part. Not the feelings. The silly girl in me wants this to be something that is unique to what is brewing between the three of us. The logical woman in me, though, totally understands that these amazing men and close friends have had a fun and exciting life before I came along.

Instead of giving him a yes or no, I decide to go with, "Well, it'll be a first for me, so maybe my opinion is better left for afterward. Depending on your… performance."

Trenton tilts his head down and gives me a sultry glare. "Oh, it's in the bag then."

My pulse has steadily sped up with each whispered innuendo, but when the door opens and Hayes slips inside, it pistons so fast I palm the spot over my chest just to make sure it doesn't bust through.

CHAPTER FORTY-FOUR

The purple glow casts a shadow over Hayes's face, creating a reflection in his glasses. For the first time since meeting him, I wish he'd take them off just so I can read his expression. Only a slight tilt of his head at Trenton reveals a silent conversation between the two men.

When Trenton had ushered me in here, Hayes knew where our unplanned meetup was intended to lead. And apparently that wordless discussion between them served as some form of confirmation.

Hayes strolls toward us with not even a hint of tentativeness in his swagger. This is his domain. Tonight, like me, he's running on the fumes of lingering adrenaline.

He comes to a stop in front of Trenton and me and drops into a squat. "Close your eyes," he whispers, covering my eyes with his hand. "Let the way you feel dictate what happens, nothing else."

The lesson he'd given me in his car comes crashing back as one of them slips their fingers through mine over the top of my hand. Instead of placing my palm over a gearshift, though, this time it's placed on something else. Something equally hard and protruding. The main differences? This shaft is warm and covered in the rough material of jeans.

Only when I squeeze, accepting the challenge and answering a silent yes to his silent question, does Hayes move his hand from my eyes.

It is Trenton directing my grip when my vision focuses again. The thickness under my palm belongs to Hayes. He is no longer below me, but standing, zipper at about eye level from where I still remain on Trenton's lap.

A new, shared adrenaline now courses through our veins — administered in a slow drip with every look, every touch, every breath of anticipation.

I let my hand fall from Hayes, stand, and walk several steps backward from them. My attention moves from one to the other, trying to give them both equal regard, as I start a slow strip tease. Not the dancing type, just the type where I take my time, seeing as I only have three items of clothing on.

Plus, this gives me a chance to figure out what, exactly, I want to do with them.

Slipping my fingers under the hem of my shirt, I wiggle it up nice and slow until there's nowhere else to go but over my head. In that motion, I pull my hair through, letting it fall over my shoulder, before tossing the shirt onto the weight bench.

Hayes adjusts his ever-growing girth. Trenton leans forward, dangling his hands between his knees as he watches attentively.

I close the distance between Hayes and me and turn around. His fingers drift across the back of my neck, brushing the strands of hair that had fallen to the center of my back over my shoulder.

When his fingers draw a line from my neck down between my shoulder blades to my bra closure, Trenton's hand snakes up my ribcage, and my stomach trembles under his touch — just how he had mentioned it responding when we were together before.

As soon as the bra loosens, Trenton's fingers are under the material and circling around my nipple in a heartbeat. Hayes inches each strap down my arms. Warm, soft lips meet the top of my shoulder, following the slow motion of the material as it descends.

The sensation of having both men stroke me in different ways at the same time makes my nipples peak and breasts flush and swell with a need for more.

Trenton removes the bra completely and tosses it near my shirt. Hayes's fingers wrap around my shoulders, and he tugs me in snugger against him.

I run my palm down my stomach and dip my hand beneath the waistband of my shorts. When the pads of my fingers meet my center, Trenton groans. Eager to get a front row visual of what I'm doing beneath the fabric, his hand drops to the button of my shorts.

All this while, when I'm not distracted and utterly lost under their watchful gazes, I make a plan.

Based on their responses already — based on this being my first time doing something with more than one guy at the same time — they're letting me run the show. Letting me decide what I am comfortable with. Which is quite a lot at this point.

Trenton works my shorts down easy, our eyes meeting and his lips twisting into an appreciative smirk in regard to my clothing choice — or lack thereof, rather.

Now that he has a better visual from his vantage point, I dip my finger lower, slipping through my entrance.

Hayes's hands come to my waist, and I use that opportunity to turn around in his arms. Trenton's hand slips around my hip and replaces mine, freeing up my fingers so I am able to unbutton Hayes's pants and aid in lifting his shirt off.

I'd seen Trenton in all his gorgeous glory, but I had yet to see Hayes. While Trenton rubs slow circles against my swollen and aching nerves, Hayes and I work together to remove his clothing. First his pants and briefs, then his shirt.

His erection bounces against my midsection, and I rise onto my tip-toes. The motion makes Trenton's fingers leave my center. Instead, he cups each ass cheek and moves his hands over the mounds and up my back, only to dip down and do the same motion all over again. Mouth reaching for Hayes's ear and center aching to feel the tip of his cock slip between my thighs, I whisper, "We really should stop bumping into each other."

He lets out a low groan and quiet chuckle. "Mm… do we?" he repeats the same playful question from earlier. I pull back a little and run my hands over his chest before taking a step back and soaking the rest of him in.

I had thought Trenton's build was pretty impressive. But under the nerdy shirts and loose jeans, Hayes's body is amazing. With a hard swallow, I turn toward Trenton and take his hands in mine. Then, I wordlessly convince him to lie down on the bed, head near the edge by the corner where Hayes is standing, feet toward the wall.

Once Trenton is on his back, I climb onto the mattress and straddle his hips, but instead of staying there, I knee-crawl toward his face. He groans and grasps the outsides of my thighs with his hands to encourage me forward faster.

I reach out to Hayes and, after he wraps his fingers around mine, coax him closer.

When my knees are at the edge and I am centered over Trenton's mouth, I descend on both men; my tongue draws a line from balls to tip along Hayes's length as Trenton's tongue runs from pussy to clit.

A mix of growls and groans hum from both men.

Legs trembling, I use Hayes as support by placing each of my hands on his hips while Trenton wrecks me with his tongue.

The creak of the door has all three of us freezing.

When Trenton's eyes shoot sideways, tongue impaled inside me, and Hayes's muscles tighten under my palms, it becomes evident that Crow's arrival is unexpected and unusual.

To them.

To me… tonight is all about firsts anyways. So, I press my center against Trenton and loop my tongue around Hayes, all the while attempting to keep my gaze locked on Crow.

He stalks to the weight bench, picks up my clothes, and sits down, straddling about mid-bench. After placing the clothes behind him, he leans forward, tattooed fingers templed at his mouth.

His steely eyes are a hazy purple under the glow of electronics, but it does nothing to remove the dark heat as they take in every slow bob of my head and shake of my thighs.

CHAPTER FORTY-FIVE

From the bench, Crow has prime view. Both Hayes and Trenton are unable to see him from their positioning. When he stays quiet and chooses to stick around, Hayes and Trenton share a quick look and Hayes shrugs.

Trenton flicks my clit with his tongue, and my fingers dig into Hayes's stomach, thighs clenching. Having the swell of a cock filling every recess of my mouth doesn't seem to deter my straying gaze, though.

My attention floats toward Crow. When our eyes lock and I glide up and back down, his fingers weave together into a combined fist, and he bites down on one of his knuckles in silent approval.

Hayes collects all my hair that had fallen in a curtain around him, gathering it into a tight ponytail in his grip. He might not be able to see Crow, without stealing a glance over his shoulder, but he still considers his presence, opting to hold my hair in his left hand and let his right arm rest at his side rather than risk blocking Crow's — and my — view.

With so many of my senses triggered and heightened, focusing on any one thing becomes increasingly difficult. Knowing Crow is the only participant distanced from the scene, I choose to focus primarily on him while letting my body give in to the mix and churn of everything else.

That idea quickly changes, though, when Trenton adds a tease of teeth against my clit, and my body takes over: my eyes close, breathing accelerates, and a moan vibrates through me.

"Damn," Hayes groans. "Make her moan around me like that again."

Trenton responds with a warm, breathy chuckle, and goosebumps spring up all over my body. His mouth is too busy writing a story with the tip of his tongue along every nerve of my clit to deliver an answer beyond that, though.

Hayes's hand follows the twist of my head as I attempt to continue. However, Trenton is determined to meet the request, and he slides a finger inside me. Nice and slow with the first, agonizing thrust. A moan is exactly what both men are rewarded with.

Heaving around the taunt of an orgasm, I drag my teeth along Hayes's length, procuring a hum from him in return. Once I'm better in control, and Trenton has moved into a rhythmic drive of his finger, I angle a look up at Hayes's face as I descend on him again. The hand he'd nicely left hanging at his side for Crow's benefit, comes up to stroke the bulge of his cock when I press it to the inside of my cheek.

He meets my gaze through his glasses, bottom lip held snug with his top teeth, and the tick of a sexy grin lifts the side of his mouth.

Trenton's finger twists and curves inside me, and I move my gaze back to Crow. In one of his signature moves, his hands have now separated and one cups his jaw while his eyes strip me down to my very soul. A tremor courses through me, and my pulse starts to pound harder, creating a staccato in my ears.

His other hand had been lying loosely atop his thigh, but when he sees that I am watching again, he brings both hands to the waistband of his jeans and tugs them off, kicking them to the side in a couple of quick motions.

His cock bounds free, and his tattooed knuckles wrap around it, all the while those steely eyes never once leave mine.

He strokes from tip to base, enlarging his length in display and challenging me all at once.

I work Hayes slowly and thoroughly until my lips meet his body and eyes water with the effort. Crow pumps again as I blink away the wetness clinging to my lashes. His eyes track slowly across our group as I deepthroat Hayes, pulling another delicious groan from his chest.

Again my eyes water from the effort, but this time my gag reflex kicks in, too, and my stomach jerks.

Crow's fist tightens and pauses, and his tongue snakes out to drag across his labret piercing.

The warmth of Trenton's mouth and pressure of his fingers leaves my center and my eyebrows curve inward.

Whatever minute amount of control Crow had lost, returns and his lips twist into a smirk. Apparently he loves to see me being tormented just as much as I love to watch him fist himself while enjoying my pleasure-agony.

Not wanting to remove myself from Hayes, I resume my slow torture, this time adding in my fingers to the mix. With the hand closest to Crow, I cup Hayes and run my tongue from base to tip again while Trenton wiggles out from between my thighs.

Approaching Hayes's side, Trenton explains with a low hum, "Since I've already had my cock buried inside you — more than once I might add — I think Hayes should get a turn."

Blinking up at him, I slip Hayes's cock out of my mouth with a pop before darting a quick glance at Crow who is still engaged in a leisurely thrust. I use this opportunity to stretch my back while Hayes and Trenton get into their new positions.

Before moving, however, Hayes bends down and places a finger under my chin to tilt my face back. Once our eyes are locked, he dips down and brushes his lips against mine before adding the press of a soft kiss. I lean into him, wanting so much more, but he backs away. After grabbing something out of a drawer, he moves around behind me, maneuvers so that his legs are between mine and I'm now situated, still facing outward but hovering above his cock with my ass against his chest instead of being over Trenton's mouth.

Trenton works himself out of his jeans quickly while Hayes rolls on protection. Now, both Hayes and I can see Crow, but Trenton is still blind to him aside from a quick, nonchalant glance in his direction mid-swap.

A pinch and dampness meets the swell of my ass. I squeak and whip my head over my shoulder, catching the top of Hayes's messy blond hair as he is bent forward and biting my flesh.

He straightens and gives me a wink while placing a hand on either side of my hips and casually lowering onto him.

Trenton leans down slightly and grasps my hand, directing me to his cock. The gentle swoop of his thumb along the string ring does not escape my notice.

When I bend forward to wrap my lips around him, he brings his mouth toward my ear. "I want you to work my cock the exact same way Crow works his."

My gaze jumps to Crow whose erection is still standing even despite his hand having stopped while he patiently waits for the show to resume.

Trenton lengthens, and I wrap my fingers around him as requested. With the first slow stroke of my fist, Hayes brings his tip to my opening, letting the motion of him filling me completely mimic the movement of my hand. The base of his cock meets my center as my palm becomes flat against Trenton's body, finger and thumb circled around him snugly.

Trenton's thighs tense at the same time mine do. Hayes guides my body up and down his shaft with a skilled grip on each of my hips.

I move a half-lidded gaze to Crow while cupping Trenton with my opposite hand. My mouth waters to consume Trenton, but I obey his request and hone in on every squeeze of Crow's fist and angling of his wrist so I can mirror everything he does.

When he realizes what I'm doing, his balls draw in tight and a small shudder twitches through him. A new shot of adrenaline infuses through me in response to witnessing him lose that bit of control. His own eyes fall to half-mast and grip tightens. In kind, I squeeze mine and earn a grunt from Trenton in return.

One of Hayes's hands leaves my hips, travels up my ribs, and cups my breast. His finger and thumb squeeze and twist lightly, sending a spear of pleasure down to my throbbing center. Trenton's hand gives my other breast the care it's heavy for, matching Hayes's pinches and rubs motion for motion while Crow engages in a steady up and down thrust, slowly increasing his pace in time with my movements.

The four of us stage this race until our bodies reach the finish line together — grunts, moans, pants, and the slapping of skin on skin are the only sounds that can be heard on the sidelines.

My entire body tenses and coils tight as I bounce maddeningly. Hayes's hand drops when he is no longer able to tend to my breasts as he loses the fight to hold back any longer.

Trenton takes matters into his own hand and raises a brow, flicking a quick glance down at my chest and back up again in silent inquiry. I give a quick nod, willing myself to wait just a second longer before exploding over Hayes. Waiting until Trenton finishes on my chest.

When his grip commits and I toy with his balls just to have continued contact with him, my eyes return to Crow. But when they alight on him, he's no longer sitting on the bench. Instead, he is now standing, chest heaving, fist pumping, teeth working his piercing.

When our eyes meet, he stalks toward me and stops at an angle beside Trenton. The two are too lost to communicate anything beyond watching and waiting for me to let go so they can let go, too.

Hayes's mouth comes to my neck, and his tongue draws a line from where my neck and shoulder meet up to my ear. "You're signaling the race, Remi. When you give the cue, we go."

A growly moan bubbles up from my chest as I clench around him. His voice, their nearness, his cock, their heated gazes… everything… everything revs me up all at once.

Hands dropping to my thighs for support as the tremble from strain mixes with the quiver of release, my pussy, thighs, and stomach clench and head falls back against Hayes's shoulder.

A groan precedes the warm wetness that spurts onto my chest. Then, another gravely grunt precedes more sticky warmth. My insides spark and combust. Hayes's fingers dig into my hips and teeth nip my shoulder as he lets out his own growl of completion.

As soon as my body finishes spasming and the high from the orgasm starts to ebb, I melt against Hayes, falling back onto my heels to give my knees and thighs a much-needed break.

He wraps his arms around my stomach and kisses the side of my neck. My eyes had closed mid-release, but I finally will them open. When I do, Crow is gathering his clothes, and Trenton is digging around for something on the opposite end of the room.

Without a word, and with only a single glance over his shoulder, Crow walks out of the bedroom, bare ass, discarded clothing bundled in his arms.

CHAPTER FORTY-SIX

A mix of guilt and anger amalgamate in my chest as the door closes behind him. The fact that it was sexy and I liked it all too much is beside the point. Doesn't a girl deserve a "Fuck, you're beautiful," or "Damn, that was hot," or "Thanks for letting me jizz on your boobs," or… hell, anything, really.

Something cool and wet presses against my chest and the image of Crow using me in the worst — best — way dissipates. Instead of Crow's silvery eyes, Trenton's sepia ones watch me intently as he wipes the mess off my chest. "Call it a lack of etiquette," he says with the half-tilt of a cautious smile. "We've known Crow since before our cocks even worked, and he's never involved himself in—"

Hayes clears his throat, cutting Trenton's words short.

"No… I get it. You've done this before and he's never joined." I fill in the blanks.

"Right. Consider it an 'actions speak louder than words,' type of thing," Trenton continues to doctor my wounded ego.

Hayes chimes in next, easing me off his lap now that Trenton has finished cleaning my chest. "That was nothing like what we've done before, with or without

303

Crow." Once we're both standing, he gives me a lingering kiss on the cheek before continuing. "Being completely in tune like that? Finishing all at the same time?" He lets out an awkward chuckle, and my heart warms at hearing a trace of the non-adrenaline-fueled Hayes as it comes back to the surface.

Trenton laugh-huffs. "Yeah, usually we're working overtime to get the girl to move past her insecurities enough to orgasm. And we refuse to come until they do. It's one of our unspoken rules."

Hayes moves to the corner of the room where Trenton had been earlier to get the cleansing wipe he used on me. Ass in full view, Hayes works to clean himself up. He looks over his shoulder and rolls his eyes, "Are you seriously talking about other women while Remi is standing right there, naked, and still recovering from what we just did?"

A laugh bubbles out of me as I walk over to the bench to collect my clothes. "It's okay. I wasn't insecure about the sex part. Just the…" Okay, so apparently talking about it brings those insecurities out a little.

I slip my arms into my bra straps and take a calming breath. The guys don't press. The room falls comfortably silent as we all start putting our clothes on. "…the attention portion," I whisper.

Part of me hopes they don't hear it; part of me wants to scream it so they do. "The feelings," I elaborate. Trenton had already mentioned it, which is why I was bold enough to bring it up now. To drive the point, I reiterate what Hayes just said: "How we were all in tune with each other." I slip my shirt over my head and work my arms through the holes. Being able to say it into a quiet room, with my back turned to the men I'm admitting this to, makes it a lot easier.

I pick up my shorts last, and slip in one foot at a time, pulling them up until I can button and zip them. "Envisioning what just happened between us, happening between you and other women. Yeah, it makes me feel a bit jealous, to be honest." Gah, apparently I become a Chatty Cathy after amazing sex. "So… anyway," I continue babbling. "Having Trenton talk about it, praising our experience over how it was with someone else… helps."

I finally turn around to face them. Both men have their eyes on me. My back had been turned, but theirs were not. They had watched every inch of clothing cover my skin just as intently as they had watched it come off.

"In that case," Trenton says with a playful gleam in his eyes, "Let me tell you about this one ti—"

Hayes punches him in the shoulder, and he grins.

Pocket insides still somewhat bunched up against my thighs, I reach my hands one by one into each to straighten them. "Maybe the campfire stories can be all about me from here on out…" My words trail as my fingers shove something crinkly deeper into my pocket. Eyebrows drawn inward, I look down and take the item out.

Hayes had been griping at Trenton, but when my focus hones in on a small yellow piece of paper, their conversation stops, and they both step forward. Several, random numbers are printed in black on the surface. I hold it up, and Trenton and Hayes shoot each other a look, both shaking their heads in a silent mutual question.

Trenton then smiles at me and says, "Guess Crow decided to give you a golden ticket. Welcome to the club." Trenton beams and waggles his brows.

"Club?" I ask, slack jawed.

Hayes rubs the back of his neck and lets out a breath. "Revelry manages a street racing club. The numbers on the tickets tell members the date, time, and coordinates."

I fold the paper up in one too many folds, until it's nothing more than the size of my thumbnail and put it back into my pocket while my heart both swells and breaks.

Such a perfect night.

Almost.

TO BE CONTINUED

ABOUT THE AUTHOR

Adell Ryan is a hubby/wife pseudonym. Adell writes unconventional love stories about fierce women and their numerous male suitors. Because let's be honest, we need more than one to satisfy our multi-dimensional needs. Right? Ryan simply puts up with Adell's crazy fantasies and toots her horn regularly. Occasionally he'll add in a shoulder pat, and a deep, sexy "Damn that's good stuff."

That southern boy (bless him) stole this northern girl's heart and they live together in the deep south, raising their three boys. When Adell isn't writing she's homeschooling — primarily working on dictation, making sure they say 'creek' instead of 'crick' and 'fire' instead of 'fer.' She also dabbles in photography and graphic design. Oh yeah, and reading. Every. Night. Much to Ryan's dismay. Sometimes she puts the steamy stuff down and gives him a quick kiss on the forehead though.

To be the *first* to know about new releases and exclusive behind-the-scenes stuff, join the fun in her FB Group: facebook.com/groups/authoradellryan/

You can also check out her website at https://www.adellryan.com and sign-up for her newsletter.

Still not enough? Find her at the listed social media platforms as well!:

Goodreads   Instagram   Pinterest
BookBub   Twitter   Patreon

Printed in Great Britain
by Amazon

42285966R00175